IT WAS ALWAYS YOU

Anna Fenwick is very fond of Matthew, a hard-working young man from her Northumberland village. She has known him all her life, although, sadly, it seems that he is not interested in her. Then Anna embarks on a whirlwind romance with Don, a visiting Canadian and goes to Calgary with him. Life is wonderful for a time. However, her heart is still in Northumberland — but when she returns to seek Matthew, will she eventually find him?

Books by Miranda Barnes
in the Linford Romance Library:

DAYS LIKE THESE
A NEW BEGINNING

MIRANDA BARNES

IT WAS ALWAYS YOU

Complete and Unabridged

LINFORD
Leicester

First published in Great Britain in 2010

First Linford Edition
published 2012

British Library CIP Data

Barnes, Miranda.
  It was always you.- -(Linford romance library)
  1. Love stories.
  2. Large type books.
  I. Title II. Series
  823.9'2–dc23

  ISBN 978–1–4448–0990–9

Published by
F. A. Thorpe (Publishing)
Anstey, Leicestershire
Set by Words & Graphics Ltd.
Anstey, Leicestershire
Printed and bound in Great Britain by
T. J. International Ltd., Padstow, Cornwall

This book is printed on acid-free paper

Anna Senses Change is Coming

She had never seen the shop looking so good. Anna gave a last look round and sighed with a mixture of pleasure and sadness. Then she began switching off the lights.

She had done everything she could. It was up to Mr Wilson now, and who knew what he would say. She really wasn't looking forward to seeing him tomorrow. She anticipated another difficult conversation.

It was still daylight when she got outside. How nice she thought. Then she smiled and shook her head. I really will have to stop being surprised every year when March comes round and it's like this again, she told herself. The change is predictable!

All the same, it was so good to come to work and go home again in daylight. When you could do that, even if it wasn't very warm, you knew spring was here at last.

As she was locking the door a voice called, 'I'm too late again, am I?'

'Oh, Matthew,' she said, turning to see a familiar face. 'Every day you arrive just as I'm leaving.'

A stocky young man with a fresh, open face and wayward hair stood smiling at her. 'I'll just have to finish the job early,' he said with a broad grin. 'If I want to eat, that is.'

Anna unlocked and re-opened the door. 'Come on in,' she said. 'Hurry up! Or the whole village will want late-night shopping.'

'It won't take me long,' he assured her. 'The first tin I see with meat in it, I'm having it. I'm starving.'

'You could do better than that, Matthew. Some of the frozen meals are pretty good these days, if you're in a hurry. But if time's not a problem, you could always buy some potatoes to peel and put in a pan to go with whatever you've bought. Has anybody ever

2

shown you how to do that? You just put some water in a bowl, pick up a knife and . . . '

'I've peeled potatoes before,' he said, laughing. 'Cooked 'em, as well. Any amount! There's nothing you can tell me about potatoes.'

'Oh, really? I am impressed.'

'We did it at scout camp.'

'Goodness! Well, if you can do potatoes, the next thing you might consider is grilling a lamb chop, and perhaps warming up a few peas. Something like that. It would be better for you than tinned food.'

'You sound like my mam. Healthy eating, eh?'

'Healthier eating — definitely.'

'I'm all for that.' Matthew smiled. Then he yawned and stretched. 'Another day, maybe. I'm too tired just now. It's been a long one.'

'Where have you been working?'

'Up on the Border Ridge, near Windy Ghyll.'

'Cold up there?'

He nodded. 'Just a bit. On the hands. The snow didn't help either.'

'Snow?'

'For an hour or two. The visibility was so bad I kept hitting my thumb with the hammer.'

Anna laughed. But she felt for him. Matthew was a self-employed fencer. He was out in all weathers, sinking posts, stringing wire, hammering nails.

It wouldn't have been much fun on his own today in the high hills.

'Here,' she said, reaching into one of the freezers for a ready-made meal. 'Try this one. It's not bad, and you'll be able to get it ready in no time.'

Matthew took the packet and read the description. 'Italian, eh?'

She nodded. 'Lasagne. It's good. I've tried it myself.'

Matthew nodded judiciously. 'Well, Italian food didn't do those Romans any harm when they were here, did it?'

'When they were building Hadrian's Wall, you mean?'

'Day and night, they must have

worked. Mind you, they had to do something to keep the Scots out. You know what they're like. They'd have pinched all the wine the Emperor brought from Italy.'

'That's character assassination!' Anna laughed and shook her head. 'It's a good thing I'm used to you. Anyway, the Scots in my family only drink whisky.'

Matthew grinned and said he'd take the lasagne.

'Another night,' Anna told him, still chuckling, 'I'll have to come round and teach you how to cook for yourself.'

'I'd like that, Anna,' he said, looking at her very seriously now, solemnly even. 'Very much,' he added.

'I bet you say that to all the girls.'

'Anna!' He looked pained. 'It would be nice. You could do some cooking while I'm watching the football on the telly.'

Anna laughed again and gave him a push. 'Matthew Greig — get out of here!'

Matthew walked home with her. It wasn't far. Anna lived with her parents in a stone-built house on the main street, at the far end of the village.

'One of these days,' she said, 'I'm going to do what you've done, Matthew, and find myself a nice little flat. It must be lovely, having your own place.'

'You haven't seen my flat,' Matthew responded with a chuckle. 'You couldn't exactly call it lovely. More like a dump.'

'It is your own place, though.'

'There is that,' he agreed. 'And I wouldn't want to be living out on the farm still. It's too remote. I have enough of that during the day.'

'It'll be nice out there at this time of year, mind, with all the new lambs skipping about.'

'Aye, it is. It's a very busy time, as well. I'll have to go and help the old man at the weekend. He'll be run off his feet again with the lambing. So will Mother.'

He sighed and added, 'Really, I should have stopped my work for a couple of weeks and gone and helped them full time. But I've got an urgent contract I couldn't put on hold. You do that once, and they don't come back the next time they want something done in a hurry.'

Anna nodded. She understood. Working for yourself, you couldn't pick and choose what work you did, or when you did it. Especially if you were a one-man band, like Matthew.

She also knew full well how busy Matthew's parents would be at this time of year. They had a farm a few miles away, up in the hills, and they would be working day and night until the lambing was done. Frost, rain, snow didn't matter. The lambs didn't hang about.

'It's a pity, though,' Matthew added. 'I'd have liked to go to the ceilidh in the Memorial Hall on Saturday.'

The dance was one of those occasional events that were much anticipated in the local community. They brought people together, often from considerable distance.

'Perhaps you'll be able to get away for the evening?' Anna suggested.

'Maybe.' Matthew's tone made it seem doubtful. 'Are you going, Anna?'

'Me?' Anna smiled and shook her head. 'I don't think so.'

'Why not?'

She shrugged. 'It's not my sort of thing.'

'Oh, you should go! There'll be plenty going on. People will be coming from miles around. Just like the old days. Besides, the hall needs a new roof.'

'That's true.'

This time the ceilidh was a fund-raiser for a new roof for the village hall.

'What do you think?' he pressed.

'Maybe. I'll see what I feel like.'

'Good!' Matthew smiled and added, 'If I make it, I'll have you up for The Light Fantastic.'

'Oh, that's far too modern for Callerton.'

They reached Physic House, and separated. Matthew continued on his

8

way, with a farewell wave.

Belatedly, she wondered where he was going. If he was going back to his flat, he was going a long way round. She shrugged and opened the front door.

★   ★   ★

'I'm home!' She paused and listened. No reply, but plenty of noise. She smiled. The sounds from the kitchen told her there was nothing to worry about. She hung up her coat and made her way through to see what was cooking.

'Hello, dear!' Her mother turned and smiled. 'You're just in time.'

'Late as usual, you mean,' Dad grumbled. 'I'm starving.'

Anna grinned. 'You don't look it, Dad. You really don't. Have you ever thought of getting some of those trousers with the elasticated waist — for comfort? Mr Wilson wears them all the time.'

Dad scowled with mock ferocity. 'If I have to wait much longer for my tea, I'll be eating this chair leg.'

Anna laughed and turned away. 'Anything I can do, Mum?'

'No. Sit down, love. Everything's ready now.'

A casserole dish arrived on the table. Everyone sat down. The campaign began.

'Actually, you are a bit late,' Mum said as she spooned food on to Anna's plate. 'Did you get held up at the shop?'

'Just for a few minutes. Matthew Greig arrived as I was locking up.'

'He seems to make a habit of that.'

'It's his work. He can't get away any earlier.'

'Tell him to do his shopping on a Saturday,' Dad said. 'Do it once a week, all in one go.'

'But it's much better to have fresh food every day,' Mum pointed out.

'Well, you're right there.'

Anna smiled to herself and kept quiet. She didn't think that was it at all.

Fresh food? Matthew was someone who rarely thought of food until he was already hungry, and by then it was too late to do anything but warm up a tin.

'I think Matthew usually works Saturdays,' she said.

'Probably.' Dad paused and thought for a moment. 'Is he still with Eddie Cummings?'

'No. He works for himself now.'

'Good for him! Well, he always was a worker, Matthew. Like his father. Still building fences, is he?'

'Yes, as far as I know.'

'Matthew's a nice boy,' Mum said, shifting the focus. 'He always was. I'm surprised he's not married yet.'

'Not everyone wants to marry these days, Mum,' Anna decided to point out. 'Not soon anyway.'

'He's getting on, Matthew.'

'Mum! He's no older than me. We were in the same class at school.'

'I do know that, dear. All I'm saying is — ' Mum paused and looked meaningfully at her.

'He wants to keep out of it as long as he can,' Dad intervened. 'If I knew then what I know now — '

Anna giggled. Mum looked cross.

'All I mean,' Dad qualified, 'is that getting wed's a fool's business, these days. The Government's seen to that.'

'Which government, Dad?'

'All governments! All we've ever had. Since — since I don't know when. There's no tax advantage at all now, whereas — '

'Honestly, you two!' Anna protested, torn between irritation, indignation and laughter. Perhaps despair, as well. 'Just for once, it would be so nice if we could complete a meal without one of you going on about marriage, and making me feel guilty because I'm not married yet.'

'Anna!' Mum said. 'That's the last thing I would ever want to do.'

'But it is what you think, isn't it?'

'Well — '

Anna watched her struggle with her feelings. 'Sorry, Mum,' she said gently.

'It's been a difficult day.'

Mum nodded and gave her a wan smile. 'I just want you to be happy,' she said.

'I am happy!'

'What about your job?' Dad asked, anxious to change the subject.

Anna grimaced. 'I don't know. Mr Wilson's coming in tomorrow morning. I'll have to see what he says.'

'It's a real shame! All the work you've put in.'

'And the village needs the shop,' Mum added. 'What will we do if it closes?'

'People should think of that every time they go off to shop at these big out-of-town stores,' Anna said, 'or order a home delivery. I feel very sorry for Mr Wilson. He's done his best. We all have,' she added sadly.

'We're Going to Have to Close'

Anna got to work a little earlier than usual the next morning. There wasn't a lot to do but she wanted to be there, just in case.

As the clock moved on towards nine, her eyes strayed constantly to the window, and the street beyond. She was nervous. She sensed this might be a big day.

The village was busy. No tourists, of course, at this time of year, but there were plenty of visitors from outlying areas. Some were headed for the doctor's surgery. Others were still bringing children to school.

Vans and trucks were collecting men and moving them out for a day's work in the woods or on the roads, in the fields or on the moors. Callerton was busy.

The ways people had found to make

a living in this little village had always amazed her. There were commuters, mostly with jobs in Alnwick, or even as far away as Tyneside, but most people of working age worked locally. Most men, at least. It was more difficult for women than for men to find local employment.

Her own father travelled round the district doing things for sheep and cattle. For their owners, rather. Selling feed supplements, and such like, Anna vaguely understood.

For a moment she toyed with the question of how he could possibly persuade sheep and cattle that there were better things to eat than grass. It wouldn't be easy. Dad earned every penny, she thought with a smile.

Matthew Greig had an even tougher job. He was outdoors in all weathers, unless he was sheltering in that old truck of his. It couldn't be much fun out on the hills in driving sleet or gale-force winds, knee-deep in February mud or working in the gloom of

November. There were days in summer that were nice enough, of course, but there weren't enough of them.

She didn't envy Matthew at all. She respected him, though. He was fun, too. She smiled as she thought of him. Even if he was a regularly late customer, she was always glad to see him. He had a good sense of humour and a ready smile. Nice-looking, too.

As Mum had said, it was a wonder some girl hadn't snapped him up by now. It wasn't as if Callerton was awash with eligible young men who worked hard, lived decently and were good company.

She sighed and thought with a smile what a pity it was he didn't seem interested in her.

She was distracted by the squeal of brakes and the sight of an enormous 4-by-4 vehicle being manoeuvred clumsily to a halt on the empty road outside the shop. She winced as it bounced over the kerb and she forgot all about Matthew. Someone more important to her right now was here.

'Morning, Anna!'

'Good morning, Mr Wilson. I see you're getting used to the new car.'

'Don't start me on that!' Mr Wilson scowled in response to her grin. 'I wish I'd never bought the stupid thing. There was nothing wrong with my old Land Rover. Nothing at all. I can't think why I did it.'

Anna could. Mrs Wilson had tired of seeing 'that old thing', as she invariably put it, parked outside their modern bungalow. Mrs Wilson had wanted to see something newer and shinier — and more expensive, as her husband had put it. Mrs Wilson had prevailed, as she usually did.

'Busy this morning, Anna?'

'Not really.'

Not at all, in fact. Mr Wilson nodded, clearly unsurprised.

'It is a bit early,' Anna offered.

'Early or late, it doesn't make much difference, does it?'

'Not in the first part of the week.

17

Friday and Saturday are our best days.'

Mr Wilson didn't respond. He glanced around the shop and began to wander, eyeing the display cases and the promotion stands, peering closely at the tinned vegetables, picking up a jar of peppercorns.

'Sell many of these?' he asked, waving the jar at her.

'Not a lot, no.'

'We should have dropped it. Dropped all them spices and herbs. They never did sell.'

'They're good to have, for when people run out.'

Mr Wilson shook his head. 'No point stocking stuff people don't buy. We should concentrate on what they do buy.'

Anna kept quiet. She couldn't imagine what he had in mind. Nothing sold well. Absolutely nothing! If they went down that road, they would stock nothing at all.

'The shop looks nice, though,' Mr Wilson added, nodding approval. 'Very tidy and clean. You've done well, Anna.'

She felt a faint stirring of hope. 'The trouble is,' he added, immediately quashing that hope, 'the shop's not making any money, is it?'

'Some weeks.'

'Oh, I know what you're going to say,' Mr Wilson said hurriedly, holding up his hand. 'And it's not your fault. Not at all. You've done far, far better than I ever expected. Better than anyone could have expected.'

There was a double-edged compliment, Anna thought wryly.

'All the same, business is business. A shop that's not making money is no good to anyone, is it?'

'It's good for the village,' Anna said doggedly. 'People would miss it.'

'Well, let them pay for it.'

'It's not exactly losing money, is it?'

'Some weeks it is.'

'Once or twice maybe. But we do quite well usually.'

She could see he wasn't listening. His mind was made up. Or Mrs Wilson's was.

'I'd like to try a few different things,' she said desperately. 'See if that helps.'

'Like what?'

'Well — ' Here it was. Not exactly a great opportunity, but an opportunity nevertheless. 'Fresh bread would do well. We could pick it up first thing in the morning from the bakery at — '

'We wouldn't sell enough. And it wouldn't keep. The sliced bread is what people want.'

'I thought we could offer a dry cleaning pick-up service for people who can't get into town themselves.'

'No money in that.'

Anna swallowed hard and kept going. 'Newspapers, I thought. And magazines. Maybe even a post office.'

'At my time of life, Anna?' Mr Wilson chuckled. 'Mrs Wilson thinks I work too hard as it is! No. What I want now is the easy life.'

'Little things, then,' Anna persisted. 'Things we don't do now.'

He looked at her.

'More fresh food, for example. Some

people in the village don't have cars and can't manage the bus ride into town, not frequently, but they still like fresh food. Or they would if they could get it. All we have, really, is tinned and frozen food. I'm sure we could do something about that.'

She'd lost him. She could see that. His mind was on other things. He wasn't interested. She wanted to get hold of him and shake him. He was hopeless. No wonder the shop wasn't up to much.

'It's no good, Anna. It isn't, is it?' He smiled and waited, waited perhaps for her to agree.

She stared stonily at him.

'I know how hard you've worked, Anna. I do know that. And I appreciate your honesty and reliability. Right from the start I've been able to trust you, and that counts for a lot these days. Everything, really.'

He meant it. She could see that. He was a kindly man, and he was being honest with her. Her steely resolve weakened.

'But it's no good,' he continued. 'The shop's not paying it's way. Mrs Wilson does the books, as you know, and she's said for a long time that the shop's not worth it.'

Mrs Wilson! Anna thought bitterly.

'So what are you saying, Mr Wilson?'

'We're going to have to close. At the end of the month. I'm sorry, Anna. But you'll find something else, something a lot better to do, I shouldn't wonder. A young woman like you? There's many an employer would give an arm and a leg for someone like you.'

He meandered on about how he would give her a wonderful reference, and what not, but Anna had switched off. He had spoken the words she had dreaded but had known would come.

The shop was to close. It had been her life for five years. She didn't know what she would do now.

Concerns About the Village

That's it, then, she thought after Mr Wilson had gone. The end of the month. Then I'm finished here, and on the scrap heap. And this is finished, too, she added, looking round the shop. All this. Gone.

Suddenly it was too much. She retreated into the back room, the stock room. She sat on a carton of cornflakes and put her head in her hands. She pressed her fingers against her face, but it was no good. She couldn't stop them. She gave way to tears.

All these years she had invested in this place. Years when she could have been doing something else. Anything else! Something useful, with a future.

The village needed her, as well. It was all right for the Wilsons, with their money and their big, fancy car, but what about some of their customers?

Old Mrs Campbell, for instance. She wouldn't be able to travel into town. It was as much as she could do to shuffle the fifty yards to the shop. And that was on a good day, when she was feeling up to it.

It would be no good talking to her about home deliveries from the big supermarkets in the town either. Even if Mrs Campbell was given a computer, she wouldn't know what to do with it. She would want to be using it to boil a kettle!

Mrs Campbell wasn't the only one, bless her. And without the shop, they wouldn't be able to survive in the village. They would probably have to go into a home somewhere, and leave this place where they had lived all their lives. Nothing to do but play bingo all day!

Anna smiled ruefully and sat up. She wiped her eyes with the back of her hand. Then she rummaged in her coverall pocket for a fresh tissue.

It was so sad and disappointing that

it was going to end like this. Infuriating, as well. But it wasn't the end of the world. Something would come up. She would find another job. Somewhere, somehow, she would. It just meant ideas of getting her own place to live would have to be put on hold for a while. That was all.

The door bell jangled. She jumped up out of habit. For a moment she contemplated sitting back down again, but she couldn't do it. Her pride wouldn't let her.

It was old Mrs Ferguson from across the street.

'Good morning, Anna! Have you got any fresh bread?'

Anna winced and glanced automatically at the rack of sliced bread. 'I'm afraid not, Mrs Ferguson. But those loaves only came in a day or two ago.'

'He'll have to have toast, then,' Mrs Ferguson said, referring to her husband, and turning to inspect what was on offer.

'You could go into town to get some?

Stay overnight and make a holiday of it!'

'At my age?' Mrs Ferguson chuckled at the thought. 'Even if I could get up the steps onto the bus, I'd never be able to get off again. Anyway, I'm not going there again till I've got some money to spend.'

Anna smiled. 'I know how you feel. You see all those lovely things in the shop windows. Then you end up buying what you can afford — a bus ticket home!'

Mrs Ferguson laughed and counted out the money for the bread. 'All the same,' she said, 'it would be nice to have some fresh bread occasionally. I'll have to start baking it myself, I suppose.'

'I suggested bringing some in but Mr Wilson doesn't want to do that. He doesn't think we'd sell enough.'

'I'll have to start a petition. Maybe that will persuade him.'

Anna laughed dutifully. She had difficulty not telling Mrs Ferguson that by next month it wouldn't only be fresh bread you couldn't buy in the village.

The old lady collected one or two things more and headed for the door. Just before she left, she turned and said, 'I don't know what I'd do without you and the shop, dear. I really don't.'

There would be a few more thinking and saying that next month, Anna thought after she'd gone. Mr Wilson wouldn't know what he'd done until he'd closed the place. Then, hopefully, people would hammer on his front door to tell him.

★ ★ ★

'Shop!' Anna grimaced and hurried through from the back room.

Carol Armstrong was tapping the counter impatiently. 'Caught you napping, did I?'

'You did no such thing!' Anna said indignantly. 'I was just putting away some new stock.'

'That wouldn't take long. I don't

think the Wilsons believe in new stock, do they?'

'Well — Not until we've sold the old stock.'

They grinned at each other. Then Carol started laughing. 'Same as our place,' she said. 'They like their money's worth, these business people.'

'You're right there. So what can I get you, Carol? Anything? Or have you just come to annoy me?'

'Cheek! I'll have a bag of crisps, while I'm here. They'll do for my lunch.'

'Fattening.'

'Think I care?' Carol twirled round, her slim figure impressive.

'No, I don't suppose you do. I don't know how you stay so slim.'

'Worry! That's how. I worry about everything. You should try it. You can eat what you like as long as you worry about it.'

Anna laughed and shook her head. It had taken Carol to prove she could still laugh today.

'I tell you why I'm here,' Carol added. 'I was wondering if you were going to the ceilidh in the village hall on Friday night?'

'Oh, I don't know.'

'It might be good.'

'I've got such a lot on my mind, Carol. I'm not in the mood.'

'What? What have you got on your mind?'

'Well . . . ' She hesitated. Then she thought, Why not? What's the secret?

'Mr Wilson just told me we're closing at the end of the month — for good.'

'Never!'

Anna grimaced. 'It's true.'

'That's awful. What will you do?'

'No idea. He just told me half-an-hour ago.'

'Oh, Anna! That's terrible. I'm so sorry.'

Anna shrugged.

'You'll have to look on the bright side,' Carol said firmly.

'Is there one?'

'Yes! There's only one job worse than

yours, and that's mine. How would you like to be cleaning out horses all day? We should both get new jobs.'

Anna knew she didn't mean it. Carol loved horses. Looking after them was what she had always wanted to do.

'You'll find something soon,' Carol added, seeing Anna's wan smile. 'You'll see.'

'I hope so,' Anna said. 'I really do. But I've been here such a long time. It will be a wrench to leave. Besides, the village needs this shop. It's the only one there is. When it closes, there'll be nothing left. No shop, no post office, no pub, no garage — nothing! Just the church, and I don't suppose that will last much longer.'

'The village!' Carol said with a snort of derision. 'It's yourself you want to think about for once.' After a pause, she added, 'Come on Friday. It'll take your mind off things. Do you good. I'll get the tickets.'

Anna looked up and shrugged. 'All right,' she said with a weary smile. 'I need a good night out.'

'Peggy Miller will be bringing her visitors.'

'Oh?'

'From Canada.'

'I didn't know.'

'New people!' Carol said, rolling her eyes. 'Hopefully. We certainly need some around here.'

Anna laughed. 'What about Phil?' she said, with Carol's boyfriend in mind.

'Oh, he won't mind.' She shrugged. 'I think he's lost interest in me.'

'That's hard to believe.'

'Besides,' Carol added, 'I've lost interest in him!'

★   ★   ★

Afterwards, Anna's thoughts returned to the future of the shop, and the village. She couldn't help it. They really would have nothing left here after it closed. Unless you had a car, and could drive, it would be like returning to the Dark Ages. Worse. Back then, every village had its coaching inn or pub.

All that would be left in Callerton when her shop closed would be houses, the church and the primary school. Oh, and the village hall — if they could raise enough money to mend the roof. Nothing else. It wasn't a prospect that could fill anyone with delight.

'He's a Nice Young Man'

She waited past closing time in case Matthew came in, but he didn't. In a way, it was a relief. She was running out of ideas for a more healthy diet for him.

Perhaps he'd found some for himself, she thought with a wry smile. More likely he was working late, wanting to finish the job he was working on today instead of having to travel back again tomorrow. Now the light nights were here he could do that — and collapse with exhaustion when he got home, possibly with a bag of fish and chips from the van that came round the village once a week.

Not for the first time, the door to the shop was hard to shut. Something had happened to it. Old age, probably. She stood back, gathered her strength and pulled it shut with a bang that made the glass panel vibrate and threaten to jump out onto the pavement.

She grimaced. Something should be done about it, but it was hardly worth mentioning to Mr Wilson. Not now. He wouldn't want to spend any more money on the shop. His big idea — or Mrs Wilson's — was to close it and then turn the whole building back into a house that they could sell for a lot of money.

Who could blame them, really she thought despondently. They were of an age when they needed to enjoy themselves, while they still could — assuming they hadn't forgotten how.

Mr Wilson would be quite happy in his garden, but she knew his wife wouldn't. She was wanting to go on one of those cruises she was always on about.

You saw them advertised in the Sunday papers. Perhaps a cruise every year, or twice a year? That would suit her nicely. Oh, she would have it all planned!

* * *

As she walked home a big car drew up just ahead of her, outside the Millers' house. The visitors, she thought, as the doors opened and people and suitcases emerged.

Peggy Miller, one of her friends, a young woman her own age, called to her. 'Friday night, Anna! Are you going?'

The ceilidh, she meant. Anna smiled. 'I think so. Carol's getting tickets.'

'Good! We are — all of us.'

A tall man with neatly-cut, black hair smiled at her before Peggy hustled him towards the front door. Anna smiled and nodded to an older couple who were following.

Peggy's Canadian visitors, she thought. They must be a family. Well, no doubt she would meet them all on Friday night.

Just as she reached her own house, she saw Matthew appear on the other side of the road. She waved to him.

He crossed the road, coming towards her. She waited.

'No, Matthew! I'm not going back to

the shop. I waited long enough for you.'

'That's all right. I don't need anything tonight, thanks.'

'Good!' She peered at him, surprised. 'Are you going out, Matthew?'

He looked unusually smart, dressed in navy trousers and a white shirt. No jacket, of course. A man who did what he did for a living all year wouldn't feel cold here on a fine spring evening.

'Just coming back, actually. I've been out for the day.'

'Oh?' That wasn't like him. 'A day off, eh? Lucky you.'

'A day off, yes. It wasn't exactly a holiday, though. I've been over to Longwitton, helping my aunt while my uncle's in hospital.'

'Nothing serious, I hope?'

'He says he needs an MOT.'

Matthew shrugged. They looked at one another. Their eyes met. He smiled.

'Oh, I like that!' Anna said, shaking her head and beginning to laugh.

'That's what he said.' Matthew shrugged again and laughed himself now. 'It doesn't mean much to me either, but — well, you know what older folk are like. There's always something wrong with them. What about your day?'

'The same. Nothing new. I wasn't very busy today.'

'Is it ever busy in your shop?'

'Sometimes it is.' She shrugged. 'It doesn't really matter now anyway.'

'Why's that?'

'Mr Wilson told me this morning he's closing the shop at the end of the month.'

Matthew gaped at her. 'Oh, no! He never is?'

She nodded. 'He is. It's true, right enough, unfortunately. It was a bit of a shock. But I suppose it's been coming for a while now, the way he's been talking.'

Matthew grimaced, and looked concerned. 'What will you do, Anna?'

She smiled, trying to be nonchalant about it. 'Oh, something will turn up, I expect.' But the bravado didn't work. 'I don't know,' she admitted. 'I don't know what I'll do.'

Matthew was quiet for a moment.

'What?' she said, seeing that he was thinking about something.

'What will I do about my tea every night?'

'Your tins of baked beans and Irish stew, you mean?'

He grinned. 'Just as I was thinking I could get used to that Italian you sold me, as well.'

'The lasagne? You liked it?'

'It's better than baked beans, isn't it? A lot better.'

She laughed and gave him a gentle push. 'Get away with you, Matthew Greig! You'll have me as daft as yourself.'

'Did you decide about Friday night, by the way?' he asked.

'The ceilidh? Yes. I'm going. Carol's getting me a ticket.'

'Good. I'll see you there, then.' He turned away. 'Oh, by the way, when the shop closes — '

'Yes?'

'Might you be moving away to work?'

'I sincerely hope not! But I don't know, really. I haven't thought that far ahead.'

He nodded. Something in his face made her add, 'I don't expect so, though. Not really.'

He smiled now and turned away again.

'Bye, Matthew!'

He waved over his shoulder. 'See you!'

She was still watching him, wondering why he'd asked about her plans, when she heard the front door open.

'Tea's ready, Anna,' her mother called. 'In fact, your dad's complaining it will be cold.'

'Coming, Mum!'

As she entered the house, her mother said, 'Was that Matthew Greig you were talking to just now, dear?'

'Yes. Just for a minute. He's had a day off today. He's been over to Longwitton, helping his aunt.'

'He's a nice young man,' her mother said.

'Yes. He is.'

It was true, she thought longingly, as she hung up her coat. He always had been.

Anna Makes a New Friend

Friday night came. As she got ready, Anna found herself looking forward to the ceilidh more than she had expected. It was time she had a night out.

She was becoming a very dull person, doing nothing but work and then going home. And at home she did nothing very much. Apart from what she did at the church, and with the Brownies. And the hospital visiting, she reminded herself. She did that, too, just as her mother had always done.

All the same, it wasn't exactly a vibrant social life. Not really. She ought to get out with Carol more often. Peggy, too. They did go into Alnwick together occasionally, and Berwick. Newcastle even. But not often enough.

She sighed. Sometimes she wondered if her mother might not be right to worry about her, and her prospects.

They weren't great, especially now she was to lose her job.

She suddenly smiled, thinking of Matthew and his uncle. She didn't think any of the people she went to see at the cottage hospital in nearby Wagton were there to have their health MOT done. Funny though, but no doubt he hadn't been having a wonderful time. Poor man. Maybe tonight she might find out a bit more. That was something to look forward to!

For the evening ahead, she chose a summer frock, in cream with red camellias dotted about. It was still spring, and none too warm, but she knew from experience that the village hall would be a steam bath once things got going. There would be hundreds of people there, in that old place, and with all the charging about the traditional dances required there wouldn't be any need of heating.

'Oh, my!' Carol said when Anna opened the door. 'Look at you. You're going to sweep them off their feet and knock 'em dead tonight!'

'I don't think so,' Anna said, laughing.

'That's a lovely dress. You look gorgeous.'

'Thank you, Carol. And so do you.'

There was no way she could compete with Carol, who was the most beautiful girl in the village, but she felt good as they left the house together and headed for the ceilidh.

No shop talk tonight, Anna thought firmly. Nothing about the Wilsons either. She was going to avoid those subjects altogether. She was going to enjoy herself. Tomorrow could look after itself.

★　★　★

The village hall had seen better days, and better evenings probably, but Anna doubted if it had ever seen a happier, more joyful occasion. Maybe it did need a new roof and a lick of paint. Possibly even some new windows. But it didn't need any more people — or any noisier people!

She stood just inside the doorway with Carol and they winced at one another. Then they shook their heads and laughed.

'Have you ever seen anything like it?' Carol screeched to make herself heard.

Anna shook her head. It was wonderful.

The Jimmy Turnbull Band was playing a lively tune, the accordions and the fiddles getting everyone's feet tapping. Folk were dancing, early as it was. Even the old ones were at it, perhaps fearing their legs might not be so reliable later on.

For a moment, Anna caught a glimpse of Matthew. Then he was gone, swallowed up by the crowd.

The beautiful Cummings sisters, Marie and Josie, were holding court, surrounded by a press of young farmers eager to urge them on to the dance floor.

George Armstrong, from The Queen's

Head, was running a makeshift bar in a corner of the room. He was doing a steady trade, but it wouldn't be long before he was utterly swamped and the queue was a mile long.

Peggy Miller came across and took Anna's hand. 'Come and meet our visitors,' she urged, pulling gently.

Anna smiled and allowed herself to be led through the throng to the far side of the hall, where Peggy's party had commandeered a table and some chairs.

'This is Anna,' Peggy announced during a small lull in the uproar. 'She's one of my oldest friends. Anna, this is Mum's brother and his family from Calgary, in Canada.'

A chorus of greetings ran round the table. Peggy ran through the names, half of which it was impossible to hear, and the other half impossible to remember.

Anna gathered, though, that there was an Uncle Bob and an Aunt Katy, and two of their teenage children. There was Aunt Katy's older sister.

There was also a young man a little older than herself, the one with the very black hair she had seen getting out of the car the other day. He looked nice and friendly. They all did, in fact.

They were a happy family group that in a little while, Anna learned, would become considerably bigger.

'Mum and Dad have gone up the valley to fetch my cousins from the farm,' Peggy said. 'They'll be here soon. With Aunt Jean,' she added with a grimace. 'They're picking her up, as well.'

Anna smiled. Peggy didn't get on with all of her relations. Aunt Jean was a particular struggle.

'You're going to have a houseful,' Anna said. 'How long is everyone staying?'

'The Canadians are staying for a month, but I like them a lot. Aunt Jean is staying for a whole night,' she added, eyes rolling with despair.

Anna laughed. She would have liked

to talk to Peggy's visitors, but it was difficult. They were sitting down and she was standing up. Anyway, the noise level made it difficult even to hear Peggy, who was standing beside her.

She glanced round, looking for Carol, who had disappeared. No doubt dancing already.

She caught another glimpse of Matthew, who seemed to be enjoying himself on the dance floor. She was glad about that. He worked far too hard.

'Can I interest you in this next dance?' someone shouted in her ear.

She turned. It was the young Canadian man, Peggy's visitor. She smiled and nodded.

'I'm Anna,' she said.

'I know. Peggy told me.'

'But I didn't catch your name.'

'Don, Don McKinnon.'

She followed him on to the floor, squeezing through the crush.

'I have no idea what this next dance is about,' Don said, turning to her.

'Neither do I,' she confessed. 'Oh, wait a minute! I think I heard them say it's Strip the Willow. I do know that one.'

'So what do you do?'

'You just charge up and down the hall, basically, when it's your turn, while everyone else claps. If you can, you whoop loudly at the same time.'

'Yeah?'

'We'll just do what everyone else does,' she assured him. 'You'll soon get the hang of it.'

And so they did. With only a few wrong turns, Don soon did get the hang of it. Especially the whooping bit.

'I can do that real good,' he assured her. 'Where I come from, it's part of our culture, our birthright. Stampede country — The Calgary Stampede?'

'Oh, yes,' she said vaguely. 'I think I've heard of that.'

'This dancing's something else, though. At home we just do disco usually.'

'So do we,' Anna assured him. 'But once in a while an old-time ceilidh like this pulls everyone together — or out of the woodwork!'

'I can see that. You dance real good, Anna,' he said earnestly.

'Oh, we learned all these dances at first school. We've known them all our lives nearly, even if we young ones don't do them so much.'

'You should. They're fun.'

'Only if you're in the mood!'

The music started up again, and they were off once more. Don really was a hopeless dancer, she decided. Clumsy, awkward, out of step with the music. But he was good looking and beautifully dressed, and he was fun to be with. He laughed a lot. So did she, she realised.

'It reminds me of Stampede,' he said during a break, when they were sitting round the table with the others.

She smiled. 'That's the rodeo, isn't it?'

'Only the biggest in the world. People dress Western all week, and there's music and dancing all over town.'

49

'Party time, eh?'

'Exactly. You'd love it.'

She wondered about that, but she nodded and smiled, and listened, as Don told her about Calgary and Stampede week.

'A million people having fun,' he concluded.

Peggy leaned over and said, 'Our kind of place, eh, Anna?'

Anna laughed. It did sound fun.

★　★　★

Later, on the way to the ladies, she saw Carol and Matthew dancing a waltz, and she stopped for a moment to watch. They looked good together, she thought enviously.

In fact, they danced better than anyone else on the floor.

Carol caught her eye and waved. Anna waved back. Matthew turned and laughed. She smiled at him.

Oh, how happy we all are tonight, she thought, continuing on her way. Tonight she would even have been able to find it within herself to be nice to the Wilsons.

They weren't here, of course. She didn't think she had ever seen them at a function in the village. They were not that sort of people.

★ ★ ★

Later still, Don walked home with her. It was a lovely spring evening. The light had lasted until late. It was cool and clear now, and a welcome change after the hothouse of the village hall.

'The air is so wonderful, isn't it?' Anna said.

'It sure is. It reminds me of springtime at home.'

'Will it be spring there, too?'

'Not quite. But winter's coming to an end. In a few weeks the ice will be breaking up on the rivers and the temperature rising. Then we'll have four months of glorious summer.'

'No rain?'

'Not much. Just the occasional thunderstorm.'

'Sounds nice.'

'Yes. You'd like it, Anna.'

'I'm sure I would.' She smiled and added, 'You must tell me more.'

An Interesting Journey For Anna

'I didn't see much of you at the ceilidh, Matthew. Did you enjoy yourself?'

'It wasn't bad.'

Matthew was inspecting the contents of the cold-storage unit, seemingly unable to make up his mind whether to buy frozen sausage-and-mash or frozen mince-and-onions.

'I saw you dancing with Carol,' Anna said.

'Yeah? You seemed to be getting on all right with that big bloke.'

'Don — Peggy's cousin from Canada? Yes. He's very nice.'

Matthew nodded. But he didn't seem his usual cheery self. Something troubling him, perhaps? She wondered what it was.

'I thought I was going to get a dance off you, Matthew?'

'What?'

'At the ceilidh. You said you would ask me to dance.'

He turned to her and shrugged. 'I couldn't get a look in,' he said. 'You were too busy.'

'That's not true! More like Carol wouldn't let go of you.'

Matthew grinned at last. 'Aye, well. There's something in that. If only she didn't have a regular boyfriend.'

'Phil? Oh, don't let that put you off, Matthew.'

He yawned and stretched. 'Anyway, she's not my type.'

'Oh, really? So who is?'

'I'll have these,' he said, coming over to the counter.

She smiled and turned to the cash register, letting him off the hook.

'Are the Wilsons still closing this place?'

'At the end of the month. I've got another couple of weeks yet. And so have you — before you have to shop somewhere else.'

'What are you going to do?'

She shrugged and gave him his change. 'No idea yet.'

He hovered, indecisive. 'What are you doing tomorrow, Anna?'

'Tomorrow? Well, for once, I'm having a Saturday off. I've arranged for Fiona Tait to look after the shop for me.'

'I know that. So what are you doing?'

'I thought I might. You know that? How do you know?'

'I'm going over to Longwitton again,' he said, ignoring her query. 'Do you fancy coming with me? Have a day out?'

She was surprised. 'How do you mean, Matthew?'

'Have a day out with me. Change of scene for you. We can have lunch somewhere along the way.'

Now she was really surprised, and confused. Was this a date he was proposing, or did he just want company to visit his sick uncle in hospital?

'I'll not ask you again,' he warned, narrowing his eyes to slits and looking menacing.

She laughed. 'All right! Yes, thank you, Matthew. That would be lovely.'

'Good. Pick you up at nine-thirty?'

She nodded.

'Good,' he repeated. 'There's something I want to show you.'

As he left, she wondered what it could be. Matthew was being unusually mysterious.

★　★　★

'What's this?' Anna asked the next morning.

'A car.'

'I can see that. Whose is it? It's not yours, is it, Matthew?'

He nodded and grinned. 'I haven't had it long.'

'I didn't know you had it at all. Oh, it's lovely!'

She walked round the shiny silver vehicle admiringly.

'Matthew Greig! You are such a secretive person. Why didn't you say you'd bought a new car? All I've ever seen you driving is the limousine — the one with the rusty patches and the noisy exhaust, and the piles of barbed wire and wood in the back.'

'Can't be taking a new Ford Focus to the places I work,' Matthew said complacently. 'It wouldn't last five minutes, up them rough tracks in the hills.'

'Is it brand new?'

'Nearly. Six months old. You get money off if you buy them like that. Anyway, stop your carping, and get in!'

'Yes, Matthew.'

She gave him a little curtsey as he opened the passenger door for her.

'Mmm! It smells new.'

'Wait till I've had it a bit longer,' Matthew said, grinning. 'I'll soon have it broken in.'

'Do you know,' Anna said thoughtfully as they set off, 'this is my first day out since I can't remember when.'

'You work too hard, Anna. There's more to life than work, you know.'

'Matthew Greig!' She laughed and

shook her head in disbelief. 'You're a fine one to talk.'

He flashed her a grin, and she began to relax and enjoy herself.

* * *

They travelled up the valley for four or five miles, and then climbed up the steep little road that led across the moor. From there, they could see Cheviot and Hedgehope in the distance. Nearer, the heather-clad moors shimmered in the bright sunlight. Pools of water from overnight rain, and perhaps from snow or frost melt, gleamed invitingly. Grass, bright green, grew in patches amongst the heather. There was scarcely a cloud in the sky.

Anna sighed. Matthew glanced at her. 'It's so beautiful,' she said happily.

He nodded. 'I always like coming this way. It reminds me why I live in this part of the world.'

'Instead of building kangaroo fences in Australia?'

'Or buffalo fences in Canada.'

They looked at each other and began to laugh. Anna knew then that they were going to have a lovely day.

* * *

In less than half an hour they reached Longwitton. It wasn't a place Anna went to very often but she remembered it as a simple, attractive little village. And so it was still. Matthew drew up and parked outside a cottage on Main Street, the only street in the village.

'We'll just pop in to see Aunt Dorothy first,' Matthew said.

The way he said it made Anna wonder what else he had in mind. It was far too early to be thinking about lunch.

Aunt Dorothy, a small, cheerful woman, welcomed them profusely. 'Come in, come in! Hello, Anna.'

She led them into a cosy kitchen that was obviously the hub of the house. Anna glanced around, admiring the oak dresser and table. Fresh daffodils occupied a central position in a vase on the dresser, illuminating the entire room.

'How is he?' Anna heard Matthew ask.

'A lot better, they say. He'll be coming home soon.'

'That's good. My uncle, in hospital,' Matthew said in an aside to Anna.

She nodded and smiled politely at Aunt Dorothy. She hoped it wasn't going to be a doom-and-gloom visit.

Over coffee Aunt Dorothy asked Anna if she lived in Callerton.

'Yes. I've lived there all my life.'

'Whereabouts, dear?'

'In the main street. Physic House, if you know it?'

'Of course. The old doctor's house. Oh, so you must be Jack and Hillary Fenwick's daughter?'

'That's right.' Anna smiled. 'Fancy you knowing them!'

'Oh, this part of Northumberland is still a small world. I used to go to dances with your mother, when we were young. Your dad was a fine dancer.'

Anna found that hard to imagine.

'Does he still dance?'

'Dad? Not since a cow stood on his foot.'

'I'm not surprised!' Aunt Dorothy said, laughing. 'Well, that's life, isn't it? One surprise after another.'

Anna smiled, and decided she liked Aunt Dorothy.

'Do you work locally, Anna?'

'Yes. I run the village shop.' She hesitated. 'Well. Unfortunately.'

'It's going to close,' Matthew said for her. 'At the end of the month.'

'Oh? That's a shame. So many villages don't have a shop any more these days. The powers that be must think everybody wants to spend half their life driving about in cars. Or on their computers, I suppose. So what are you going to do next?'

Anna shook her head. 'I haven't really had time to think about it.'

'I thought we'd go over to see Gordon,' Matthew said, rescuing her from what she feared might become an interrogation. 'Anything we can get you while we're there?'

'I don't think so, thank you,' Aunt Dorothy said. 'Will you be coming back for lunch?'

'No, but thanks anyway. I'm treating Anna to a meal out today.'

'Oh? Lovely!'

'Enjoy your day, dear,' Aunt Dorothy added as they were leaving.

'Oh, I will. Thank you. And I hope your husband is home soon.'

They left the car where it was, and headed across the street.

'Where now, Matthew?'

'The village shop,' he said, pointing ahead. 'Longwitton's prize-winning village shop.'

* * *

The shop was a little further along the street. It occupied the ground floor of a substantial stone house. Anna looked at it with interest.

She could see the shop front had recently been re-painted. It was dark green, with delightful little pictures — emblems, really — picked out in gold of the kind of things a village shop might be expected to stock: loaves, sausages, fish, apples, a teapot.

A name went with the shop title: *Gordon Turnbull, Provision Merchant*, written as a signature in a pleasing copperplate script.

'Oh, my!' Anna said, impressed. 'How lovely.'

She stopped to study the shop front in more detail. It was beautiful, almost an illustration from an elegant book. The windows were clean, and not obscured by posters or pamphlets.

A simple display occupied the central window: a pyramid of boxes of tea, with a bowl of fruit to one side and one of flowers to the other. Somebody had taken a lot of care to arrange something so simple and elegant. She bet the display was changed frequently.

'He doesn't have a lot in the window,

does he?' Matthew said.

'No, but he has enough. It's a very attractive window,' Anna said, the more impressed, the longer she studied the display.

'I think it's beautiful, and clever. Tasteful. I hate those shop windows where everything is crammed in on top of everything else. I've never been able to get Mr Wilson to agree that that's a poor way of doing things. He thinks you have to show everything you've got in the window, or folk won't come in.'

'Let's have a look inside,' Matthew suggested.

She wondered what he was thinking. Were they here to meet a friend of his, or part of the family? Not that it mattered, she thought, following Matthew. It would be interesting just to see inside.

The exterior of the shop might have been clear and uncluttered, but inside it was a different matter.

'Aladdin's Cave!' Matthew said with a grin.

She smiled. She knew what he meant, even if it wasn't how she would have put it. There really was a lot of stuff here, but she could see at a glance that it was well-organised. Everything in its place, all arranged by a tidy and thoughtful mind. Excellent use of the available space, in fact.

She guessed they sold almost everything. They were light on perishables — the fresh food, and so on — but there was a good range. And if you wanted a newspaper to go with your morning coffee, or a sharpener for your pencil, let alone quality marmalade or a light bulb, you would get it here. Shoe polish, as well. And small nails and screws.

In the morning, at least, there would be fresh bread — she could smell it now — and in the afternoon, a notice said, there would be a dry-cleaning collection and delivery service. There was fresh milk, of course. And free-range eggs. A surprising array of fruit and vegetables, too, and shelves holding a variety of wines and beers.

'You'll be wanting change for the parking meter, I suppose?' a man's voice called.

'A box of matches, actually,' Matthew replied. 'A small one, the smallest you've got. And will you take a cheque?'

Anna spun round to see Matthew and a man a little older than themselves laughing at each other as they shook hands.

'Anna, meet Gordon, my cousin. Gordon, this is Anna.'

Anna smiled. 'I'm pleased to meet you, Gordon.'

'From Callerton?'

'Yes,' she said. 'Born and bred.'

'I'm pleased to meet you at last, Anna. Matthew has told me a lot about you.'

'Really?'

She glanced sideways. Matthew looked embarrassed but defiant.

'That you have a shop, at least,' Gordon amended.

'Well, I manage one, but not for

much longer. It's closing at the end of the month.'

Gordon grimaced. 'It's a problem, isn't it? Village shops are struggling everywhere.'

'Are you struggling, as well?'

'Us? Not really, no. We're managing. We're an exception, fortunately.'

'You must be doing something right, then.'

'He's a prizewinner,' Matthew said, pointing to a plaque on the wall.

'*Village Shop of the Year*' she read aloud. 'Wow! I'm impressed.'

She was, too. She had read about the competitions and awards, even if she had long since abandoned hope that the Wilsons might think it worth entering their shop. Always, whenever she had proposed it, there had been some reason for it to be a bad idea.

'Thank you.' Gordon shrugged modestly. 'Coffee?'

The enticing smell was irresistible. 'Please,' she said.

Gordon broke off to serve a customer.

Then he led them to a small table in the corner and took a flask from the nearby coffee-maker.

'So how do you do so well?' Anna asked. 'I mean . . . ' She paused and waved around her. 'Apart from having such a beautiful shop!'

'We've been going a long time,' Gordon said. 'That helps. Tradition, and all that. My great-grandfather started the shop. Before that, he used to go round the district, first with a pony train and then with a horse and cart. The shop saved him a lot of shoe leather.

'The family just kept it going,' he added with a shrug.

'So you were born to it?'

'To be a shopkeeper?' Gordon laughed. 'I didn't think so. I wanted to see the world, and be a footballer or a brain surgeon. I was born too late to be an engine driver, a proper one, that is, with a steam engine. I could have been an astronaut, I suppose. At one time I thought of that.'

'The usual?' she said.

'The usual.'

'Then he changed his mind,' Matthew contributed.

'I did. You're right, there, Matthew!' Gordon laughed again and shook his head. 'After a few years of messing about, I started to help out a bit in the shop. I found I quite liked it, and I could see I could make a decent living out of it. So I took it on myself when Dad wanted to retire.'

'The rest is history,' Matthew said.

'Oh, you!' Gordon shook his head and looked sadly at Anna. 'Messing about in the hills all day, he has no idea what a real business is like.'

Anna grinned. They were obviously good pals, these two.

'Tell me what you've done,' she said, 'to make it such a success. I'm really interested.'

'It's just common-sense, basically. You can't afford to keep much in the way of things that go off quickly, but on the other hand you do have to stock the things people want. It's not really a mystery or a secret. You just have to be intelligent about it, and understand your customers — your local market.

'You know yourself, a small shop can't compete on price or range with the big supermarkets in town, but we can provide a local service. Good choice, quality, reliable, here-right-now. That's our strength. We occupy what the experts call a niche market.'

'Do you keep fresh bread?'

'We sell it — but we don't keep it. I get a delivery every morning. When it's gone, it's gone.'

'So people have to come early for it?'

'Or order it. Then we can keep it for them.'

'That makes sense.'

'But I do have a little secret contingency plan.'

'What's that?'

'I freeze some of it, as well. So if someone is too late or hasn't ordered it, a good customer, say. I can let them have a fresh loaf that's been frozen. I can always find something for them.'

'The same with milk, and so on?'

Gordon nodded. 'Yes. I have some big freezer units in the garage. So I can nearly always find something for a customer. That keeps them coming back.'

'You'll be more expensive, though?' Matthew suggested.

'Than what? The supermarket? Not when you consider that a road trip to a supermarket will cost someone five or six pounds in petrol, or half a day on the bus. Yes for a big, monthly shop, but not for small quantities or everyday things that you want right now.'

He was really on top of things, Anna thought. He knew exactly where his strengths and weaknesses lay, and he used the knowledge effectively. This was how to run a village shop! She felt quite envious.

'What about meat and fish?' she asked.

'Well, people can always have it frozen. If they want it fresh, they either take pot luck with what I have or else they order it. I'll take orders.'

'You seem to have thought of everything.'

'Not quite, but we do try.'

That use of 'we' raised another question.

'You don't do all this on your own, surely?'

'Not really.' Gordon chuckled and shook his head. 'No, it's simply not possible. It's a two-person operation.'

He looked round as the door bell clanged and another customer appeared. 'Sorry, but I need to get on. When you've finished your coffee, Matthew, why don't you see if you can find Kay? She's out the back somewhere.'

Anna Spends Time With Don

Matthew led Anna through a doorway into the house proper. 'What a nice old place,' she remarked, glancing around with interest.

'It is. Too big, though.'

'Do you think so? It seems a lovely family home to me.'

'Except there's just the two of them. They're finding it difficult to start a family.'

They found Kay in the garden at the back of the house. She was on her hands and knees, digging with a hand fork.

'What are you up to?' Matthew called.

'Hi, Matty!' she said, looking over her shoulder. 'What a nice surprise. Hello!' she added, getting to her feet when she saw there was someone else with him.

'Anna, Kay,' Matthew said, with

minimum ceremony.

'Goodness. I wasn't expecting company.' Kay got to her feet, brushing herself down. 'Just look at me!'

Anna smiled. 'Please don't mind me. You're gardening. We've just been looking round the shop,' she added.

'Gordon would enjoy that.'

'It's quite a place. I've never seen anything like it.'

'Thank you.' Kay smiled and added, 'We are rather proud of it.'

She led them over to a patio, where they sat on summer chairs that had appeared early.

'You have a lovely garden, as well,' Anna said, glancing round.

'It could be lovely, but we don't really have time for it. If you want some advice, Anna, don't ever take on a village shop. It takes over your life.'

'Too late,' Matthew said. 'She already has one.'

'Oh?' Kay looked at her with fresh interest.

'It's not mine. I just run it. Not for

much longer, though. The owner has decided to close at the end of the month.'

'That's wonderful! You'll be free.'

'Yes,' Anna said with a sigh. 'That's how I'm beginning to feel. Unemployed, but free.'

★   ★   ★

Afterwards they left Longwitton and drove on a little further, heading for Lynn Spout, a picturesque waterfall. Matthew was quiet. Anna was grateful for that. She was thinking about what they had just seen and heard. And there was such a lot to think about.

They left the car beside the road and set off on the footpath that led up through woodland to the Spout.

'The shop was what you meant, wasn't it?' Anna said eventually. 'When you said there was something you wanted me to see?'

Matthew nodded. 'I thought you might be interested.'

'Because?'

'Well — '

'Because you thought it might get me thinking?'

Matthew looked innocent. 'Who, me?'

'Don't give me that, Matthew Greig! You knew perfectly well what you were doing all along.'

He grinned but he didn't deny it. So it hadn't been a date, after all. He had just been trying to help her. Well, she couldn't complain about that. No-one else had tried to help her.

'You're wasted on fences, Matthew. You should be in Parliament.'

'And you should be in business for yourself,' he said firmly. 'Never mind the Wilsons. You should have your own shop, Anna.'

'There's a lot to consider, you know, even without thinking about the money that would be needed. It would be a big undertaking.'

'True. But you'd be good at it. And it's not as if it would be new to you.

You've been in the trade long enough. You've got the contacts. You know what to do. You're well known in the area, and very well thought of.'

All of which, except the last point, she knew to be true.

'They would help, you know.'

'Who? Gordon and Kay?'

He nodded.

'No, they wouldn't. I would be a competitor.'

'Not this far away. No-one from Callerton goes to Longwitton to shop.'

That was probably true, too. Matthew knew what he was talking about. She looked at him afresh.

'What?' he said defensively.

'You have a good business head on your shoulders, young Master Matthew.'

'Why, thank you, Ma'am!' He touched an invisible cap — or was it an invisible forelock?

She laughed and clutched his arm.

'Oh, Matthew! What a lot you've given me to think about. Thank you so much. But let's not do any more of that today. Let's just enjoy ourselves.'

'Just one thing I want you to remember,' he said.

'And what's that?'

'I'll help, as well, if I can, and if you want me to.'

She squeezed his arm in acknowledgement. She was, she realised, having to think about Matthew in a different way. He really was a businessman.

* * *

Disappointingly, she heard no more from Matthew. She had hoped, and expected, to see him again very soon after their lovely day together, but it hadn't happened.

Obviously, she decided, he had just been trying to cheer her up. He wasn't really interested in her. The shop talk had been for the same reason. Matthew being kind.

Still, it had been a nice day, and when such days came along you just had to accept them and then get on with your life.

But one day she received a surprise visitor in the shop. The clang of the door bell brought her racing through from the stock room. It was Don, Peggy's Canadian cousin.

'Oh, hello!' she said.

'Hi, there!' He chuckled at her obvious surprise. 'So this is where you hang out?'

'Every day,' she said, smiling, and refraining from adding that it was only until the end of the month.

Don was gazing around the shop with apparent interest.

'You're looking for something in particular?' she asked.

'No. I'm just wondering what you stock.'

'Not very much, I'm afraid. We're not a supermarket or a department store.'

'I can see that.' He turned towards her and smiled. 'But you must be the only shop for miles?'

'At least seven,' she confirmed. 'Some

people rely on us for their everyday needs.'

'I'll bet. Seven miles, eh?'

She nodded.

'Back home,' Don told her, 'I would happily drive twenty miles across the city to get to a place I like to shop.'

'Really? It must be a big place.'

'It sure is, and getting bigger every day.'

'Well, not everyone could do that here, even if Callerton were big enough. Some people don't have a car. Some are too old, or infirm, to drive. And some are too young!'

Don laughed with appreciation. 'And cabs are in short supply, I guess?'

'Practically non-existent.'

'Buses?'

'Much the same. You can get a bus to Alnwick some afternoons, and to Berwick every Friday.'

'As often as that? Well, folks here have no real need of a car, do they?'

She laughed. Who said Canadians had no sense of humour? Carol, probably. Or was it Peggy?

She quite liked Don. He was very handsome, with his jet black hair and olive complexion. He was a big man, too. Over six feet tall and well built. Not to mention smartly dressed, in his fashionable smart-casual clothes.

'Do you play that game — American Football?' she asked.

He shook his head. 'In Canada we play Canadian Football.'

'Soccer?'

'No. It's like the US game, but with slightly different rules and fewer men.'

'Fewer men? Why?'

'Our men are bigger. Besides, we Canadians like wide-open spaces.'

'But didn't I read somewhere that most of you live in big cities?'

'Nearly all of us. That's true. But we think we like wide-open spaces, and maybe for some of the time we actually do, at weekends, say, and on vacation.'

Anna laughed again and shook her head. 'So do you play Canadian Football?'

'Used to. At high school. Not any more, though. I don't play hockey any more either.'

'Ice hockey?'

He nodded.

'What do you play now?'

'Making money mostly.'

'Really? And you enjoy that game?'

'Very much. I aim to make enough to retire before I'm forty.'

'Goodness! You do look ahead.'

'How about you, Anna? What are your plans?'

'Oh, mine only go another couple of weeks. Then I retire. At least, I look for another job. Mr Wilson is closing the shop.'

'That's too bad. So what will you do then?'

'No idea at the moment. But something will come up, I expect.'

Don considered this and then said, 'A couple of weeks? That's a long way off. I wasn't thinking that far ahead. What are you doing this afternoon? Working?'

She shook her head. 'It's my half-day.'

'Half-day?'

'You don't know about that?'

He shook his head. She felt a need to explain the traditional custom, one still observed in Callerton.

'We're open all day Saturday. So Mr Wilson insists on me having a half-day on a Wednesday. It's old-fashioned, I know, but I don't really mind.'

Don nodded gravely, as if he found the explanation barely comprehensible. No doubt it was, she thought, to someone from a big city.

'How nice for you,' he said finally, making it sound not nice at all, which, really, it probably wasn't if you thought about it.

'In Newcastle, the big supermarkets are open twenty-four hours a day, every day of the year,' she added a shade defensively. She didn't want him thinking everything in this country was unreasonably quaint.

He nodded. 'So you're free this afternoon?'

'Free?'

'Don't have to work. It's my lucky day. Would you do me a very great favour, Anna?'

She waited, with no idea at all what to expect next.

'I need to shop for some gifts to take home with me. Could you point me in the right direction? Some place I could go? Better yet, could you come with me, to stop me getting lost or ripped off?'

She thought quickly. Why not? Anything at all to get out of the village for an afternoon. She had no problem with that.

'In return, I would like to buy you lunch. How does that sound?'

It didn't take her long to think about that either. 'Be here at one sharp,' she said. 'I'll be very hungry by then.'

'One, it is!' Don grinned and turned to leave.

★　★　★

They started off with lunch. Don was insistent that that was the priority after a hard morning's work for Anna.

'Not so hard, actually,' Anna chuckled. 'Now I can't re-order and re-stock, there's not so much for people to buy. So they don't come into the shop so much.'

'What do they do instead — internet shopping?'

'Oh, yes!' Anna laughed. 'I can just see old Mrs Campbell poring over her new laptop. So where do you want to go?'

'You name it.'

She named The Fox and Pheasant, a pub not far away that she knew served food all day.

* * *

They travelled in Don's hired car, a rather luxurious saloon that Anna guessed had cost him a lot of money. On the way they talked about life in the village. He asked her what she did when she wasn't working in the shop.

'Not a lot,' she said, feeling defensive. 'I support our church. I help out with the Brownies. I visit the old folks in the cottage hospital. See friends. That sort of thing.'

Don didn't say anything for a moment. Then he glanced at her with amusement and said, 'What do you do for fun?'

'For fun?' She gave a wry chuckle. 'In Callerton?'

'Clubs, discos, parties — that sort of thing?'

'Oh, there's not much of that here. Fun? Don't be ridiculous!'

'Well . . . '

She relented and laughed. 'Where do you think this is, Don? We live a quiet life here. Oh, we have the occasional ceilidh, like the one last Friday. People do have parties from time to time. And sometimes I go into town with friends, to shop or go to the cinema. Sometimes we go to an Italian restaurant in town. There's plenty to do, if you get organised, and if you want it.'

Don was very quiet.

'It's not a very glamorous lifestyle, I'm afraid,' she added.

He chuckled and said, 'I guess it doesn't need to be. Nothing wrong with that. I bet you're happy with things just the way they are.'

'Well — '

Moments later they arrived at their destination, saving her the need to respond, sparing her the need to list the disadvantages of living in a village like Callerton.

★ ★ ★

The Fox and Pheasant was a very old pub. Historic even. Once, it had been a coaching inn. Once, almost certainly, it had seen better days. But at least it served food. Anna just hoped she wouldn't have to apologise for the quality.

'As long as they can manage a decent burger,' Don assured her, 'I'll be OK.

Don't you worry about me.'

It was a quiet day for The Fox and Pheasant. So they chose to eat in the bar, where there were one or two people lingering over coffee and half-empty glasses, preferring that to the empty dining room.

Don gazed around with interest at the brass ornaments on the walls, the stuffed birds and animal heads, and the huge salmon that once had lived in the nearby river.

'It's quite a place,' he said, turning to her.

Anna nodded. 'Very old,' she said.

'I can see that.' He nodded and turned back to her. 'What will you have to drink?'

She chose a fruit juice — 'exotic' flavour. 'I like surprises,' she said.

Don opted for a beer. Anna hoped it would be only one beer, with him driving, and said so. He laughed and told her she was bad as his mother.

The menu was surprisingly varied. Burgers were not even mentioned. Don chose *Special Northumberland Sausage*, of which Anna had her doubts, together with what the menu card called *mash and veg*.

'I like to try local specialities,' Don said.

Anna herself chose grilled salmon and a salad. 'At least one of us should try healthy eating,' she said.

Don laughed. 'On holiday?'

'You might be!'

'OK, working girl.'

'Are you enjoying it, by the way — your holiday?'

'Very much so. It's real good to see so many members of the family, some for the very first time. And the slow pace of life here is a welcome change for me — at least for a little while.'

'Do you have a very busy life in Calgary?'

'Oh, sure. All the time. It never stops, never rests.'

He went on to tell her of his work as a lawyer in the oil industry. He seemed to be very enthusiastic about it.

'You should see the view from my office window,' he enthused. 'It's on the 38th floor of the Grant Building, right in the downtown, and you can see for almost a hundred miles in any direction. The foothills and Rockies on one side, and the prairies on the other.'

'It must be lovely,' Anna said, struggling to appreciate how anyone, anywhere, could see such distances.

'It is. You'd love it.'

Perhaps, she thought. Yes, she probably would. But she could scarcely imagine it. The less so, the more Don told her about it. What could life in such a big city be like? Compared with her own life here, his sounded as if it was on another planet.

As well as a downtown office, Don had a downtown apartment — for convenience, he said. For weekends, the family had a cabin in the foothills somewhere, and he had what he called a 'sail boat' on a lake.

He drove a sports car, of course, a Porsche, except when he drove his SUV or his BMW saloon. Holidays took him anywhere in the world, it seemed, and they occurred surprisingly frequently.

'It sounds a very, a very Californian lifestyle,' Anna ventured.

'It's way better than that,' Don assured her. 'And there isn't any place on earth to touch it.'

'So You're a Free Woman?'

Anna did like Don. More and more, she enjoyed his company, and the novelty of going out with someone on a regular basis. And they went out together a lot over the next couple of weeks. Don transformed her life.

She could think of little else but him. In fact, she couldn't wait for the end of the month and the closure of the shop. Then she would be able to spend even more time with Don. After all, he wouldn't be here for long. Just a few weeks.

Carol noticed the difference in her. 'You don't seem so worried about the shop?' she said when they met on the street early one evening.

'No? Perhaps I'm not. What will be will be, won't it?'

'That's the spirit!' Carol peered at her. 'Have you got something else lined up?'

'No, not really.'

'Not really?'

'Not at all,' she said firmly. 'I'm just taking one day at a time. Enjoying myself.'

'It wouldn't have anything to do with Peggy's gorgeous cousin, would it?' Carol giggled.

Anna nodded happily. Her secret was out. 'It might,' she admitted.

'You've been going out with him, have you?'

'Occasionally,' Anna said airily.

'I'm jealous! I saw him first.'

Anna laughed and glanced at her watch. 'Oh, sorry!' she said immediately. 'I didn't mean to do that.'

Carol smiled. 'Is that where you're going now? To see Don?'

'I'm waiting for him, yes.'

'Well, have a lovely evening, and don't you worry about that silly old shop any more. I told you something would turn up!'

That was the evening when Don first kissed her. They had been for a meal in a cosy little restaurant in Alnmouth. Afterwards they walked along the beach, hand in hand, listening to the roar of the sea and watching the lines of breakers.

'Bet you don't have this in Calgary,' Anna teased.

'No, we don't.' Don smiled at her. 'Pretty much everything else, but not this old ocean.'

He stopped and turned towards her. Head on one side, she looked at him and smiled. He leaned down towards her. She reached up to meet him.

Before she knew it, they were locked together in an embrace that seemed to last for hours.

'There's no you in Calgary either,' he said when they drew apart. 'No Anna Fenwick.'

'But there is someone else?'

He shook his head. 'No, no-one.'

He tightened his grip on her hand and they walked on across the sand.

No-one, Anna thought happily. No-one at all.

The day came. The Wilsons both came to pay her last wages, reclaim their keys, see her off the premises, and lock up the shop. Anna had been dreading this day. Now she couldn't wait to get out. This part of her life was over. She couldn't wait to move on.

'There's a lot of stuff left,' Mrs Wilson said disapprovingly, looking round at the shelves. 'Now it will be wasted. Couldn't you sell any of it?' she added, looking hard at Anna. 'All this stock is worth a lot of money, you know, and money doesn't grow on trees.'

Anna felt she was being accused of negligence or incompetence. Fortunately, Mr Wilson was more fair-minded. He responded to his wife with a mild reproach.

'Steady on, Edith. Anna's done her best. What's left wouldn't be easy to sell, even at knock-down prices. Most of the stock has gone anyway.'

Mrs Wilson sniffed and let her face show what she thought of that.

In truth, Anna thought, glancing around herself, there wasn't a lot left. What little there was still on the shelves could still be here next Christmas. Tins of shoe polish that hardly anyone used any more. Long-life bread that Mr Wilson had thought a sensible thing to stock. Tinned meals that only Matthew ever bought.

'Mr Wilson,' she said, 'I've been meaning to speak to you. I don't know what you plan to do with the shop now, but if you're interested in leasing it, as a shop still, I might be interested in taking it over.'

'Might you?' Mr Wilson gazed at her with a friendly smile. 'Not had enough of it?'

'No. I've enjoyed working here.'

'Out of the question,' Mrs Wilson snapped. 'It's closed. Finished. This is the end of it.'

Anna thought a wistful trace of regret passed over Mr Wilson's face before he spoke again. After all, the shop had been an important part of his life, too. 'I'm sorry, Anna, but Mrs Wilson is right.'

'I just thought I'd mention it,' Anna said bravely, not really disappointed with the answer she had received. It was what she had expected.

Mr Wilson thanked her for her work and wished her well in the future. He said to let him know if she ever needed a reference. Then Anna handed over her keys and said goodbye.

By then Mrs Wilson was too busy poking around in the stock room to do more than call an unenthusiastic reply, but her husband was a little kinder.

'You'll do well, Anna, whatever you choose to do. Don't you worry about the future.'

She was glad to get out after that.

* * *

On her way home she saw Matthew half-way up a ladder that was leaning against an old building that had been empty for a long time. She called to him. He looked round and waved. She watched as he poked at a window frame with a screwdriver.

'What are you up to, Matthew?'

'Oh, not much.' He flashed her a grin but carried on with what he was doing.

She waited, but he said nothing else. She watched for a few moments and then continued on her way. He was busy, obviously. Looking to repair the window, it seemed. Matthew wasn't just a fencer. He could do most things. Turn his hand to anything, people said.

She was disappointed he hadn't had time to chat to her for a moment, but that went with her day. Disappointment all the way through, until now. The evening would be different. She was seeing Don this evening. She couldn't wait.

'So you're a free woman?' Don said.

'Free? Yes, I suppose I am.'

'How does it feel?'

She looked round the restaurant

before she replied. They seemed to spend all their time together in restaurants. She had never known anything like it.

Feel? She wasn't sure what she felt. Nothing, really. Fed up, perhaps. Tired. Apprehensive.

'I suppose my life is changing — has changed already, since this afternoon, but I don't feel particularly happy about it. It's not what I wanted, or expected.'

She shrugged and added, 'I'll just have to look for another job now. That's all.'

'You don't think this is the best thing that ever happened to you?'

'No, I don't.'

She looked at him and smiled ruefully. 'Stop trying to humour me, Don. It's no big deal. I just have to look for another job. That's all.'

'Right.' He smiled back and said, 'Did I ever tell you how beautiful you are when you get annoyed with me?'

She laughed and shook her head

wearily. 'No, you didn't. And don't start telling me now either. I'm not in the mood. Besides, I'm not annoyed with you.'

What a silly man! She had to laugh, though. He was very good at taking her mind away from her everyday worries.

★ ★ ★

It was late when she got home that evening. There were lights on in the house but she thought no-one else would be up still. She tried to make no noise. She took her shoes off just inside the door.

'That you, dear?' Mum called from the kitchen.

Anna smiled. She might have known!

She went through into the kitchen. 'I thought you would be asleep by now.'

Mum yawned and pushed a magazine aside. 'Oh, I wasn't sleepy tonight. Your father was, though. He'll be snoring his head off by now.'

Anna smiled. 'Mum, you don't have

to wait up for me, you know.'

'Of course I don't. And I wasn't. Would you like some cocoa, dear?'

She hesitated. It was so late. Then she remembered she wouldn't have to be up at her usual time in the morning. So why not?

'Yes, please. That would be lovely.'

She watched her mother get up and start hunting for mugs and spoons.

'Did you have a nice evening?'

'Yes. Lovely, thank you.' Anna yawned and added, 'Don took me to a restaurant in Alnwick.'

'Which one?'

'I can't remember the name. It was the Italian one on the market place.'

'Oh, yes. Tarantino's? Something like that.'

'Yes. What did you do?'

She listened as her mother told her about visiting an old friend who wasn't well, and being visited in turn by a friend of her father's. It was last-minute seed catalogue time, as well. Time still for poring over what to grow in the forthcoming summer. The usual, in fact. An evening spent in the way people lived in the village. Boring, really.

'You seem to be seeing a lot of Don?' Mum said as they sipped their cocoa.

'Yes. He's very nice. I like him a lot.'

'Is he a proper Canadian?'

Anna laughed. 'Proper? Whatever do you mean?'

'Well, was he born there, or did he emigrate with his parents?'

'Oh, he was born there. He's lived all his life in Calgary, I think.'

'I don't remember his parents. They emigrated before I was born. But the Millers have always been a nice family. All of them.'

'Except Peggy's Aunt Dorothy?'

'Peggy's aunt. Oh, Dot Miller, you mean? She has the farm up by Dancing Hall?'

Anna nodded to encourage her. Mum chuckled. 'Dot was always difficult. Strong-minded, determined — and stubborn! She should have emigrated, as well. She would have got on well in the back of beyond.'

'That's what Peggy thinks!'

They chuckled over that. Then Mum changed the subject. 'What are you going to do now the shop's closed?'

'I don't know. Look for another job. I'll find something.'

'Round here? There's not much for you in Callerton.'

'Something will come up.'

'If you have to leave, love, Dad and I will understand.'

It was said so hesitantly, and Mum looked so sad, that Anna was almost moved to tears. 'Don't worry so!' she said, getting up to give her a hug.

She got a brief smile in return. But she could tell how worried Mum was. Given that, the last thing she could tell her was that Don had spent a lot of the evening trying to persuade her to think about emigrating to Canada.

Anna Feels Snubbed
by Matthew

The next morning Anna got up at her usual time. She had planned to have a lie-in but her mental clock was stuck in its old routine. So she was up at seven, in time to join her father at the breakfast table.

'I didn't expect to see you this morning,' he said.

'And I didn't think I would see you, but here we are, as usual.'

'Any plans for the day?' Dad asked, pouring her a cup of tea.

'Not yet. I might go into the job centre in Alnwick. Or I might just sit and watch day-time television.'

'No use feeling sorry for yourself. You'll soon get something else.'

'I hope so.'

She really did. She wasn't built for

doing nothing all day. She wasn't used to it. But she knew it wouldn't be easy. After a month nearly of making applications that had come to nothing she was reconciled to that. Very few companies and organisations advertising jobs even had the courtesy to acknowledge applications, never mind tell you what had become of them.

Besides, there weren't a lot of opportunities around Callerton anyway. Probably not in any rural area, if it came to that. Especially for someone without academic or professional qualifications.

She sometimes wished now that she hadn't been so eager to leave school and get a job. At the time, it had seemed the best thing. Now she wasn't so sure. Perhaps she should have listened to what people were telling her.

Then she could have been a teacher or a nurse by now. Or a brain surgeon, or an airline pilot. Or — or anything!

And now she had Don lecturing her on her future. Telling her what a future someone like her would have in his wonderful big city, where a million people lived such prosperous, exciting lives. It was too much, altogether too much.

* * *

Later, after Dad had gone off to work and Mum was preparing to visit someone else who wasn't well, Anna opened the front door and stepped out onto the street. Her first day of what Don had called 'Freedom'! Well, let's see what it's like, she thought. Let's see if it's all it's cracked up to be.

It was much the same as any other day, she soon decided. Callerton hadn't changed. She walked along the main street, observing what was happening. The postman was busy. There were still cars parked near the school, some mums not yet ready to be back home. A man she didn't know was walking with his dog. The little church was closed. Peggy Miller must still be at home. At least, her car was outside. Perhaps she was on holiday?

But some things were different. The shop, her shop, was closed, the blinds drawn, no lights on, no-one inside. Who said Callerton never changed?

Something else was different, too. As she approached, she could hear the sound of a power drill at work inside the old, ruined cottage where she had seen Matthew poised on a ladder. The ladder was still there, as well.

As she drew level, Matthew appeared. He was about to climb the ladder when he saw her. He stopped and waited.

'Hello, Matthew! Here again? What are you up to?'

He gestured with his head towards a window frame standing against the wall. 'I'm just fixing the new windows.'

'Someone has decided to renovate this old place, have they?'

He nodded. 'It's going to take a bit of work, mind.'

'I'll say! It's been empty many a year.'

'Forever, I think. What about you,

Anna? What are you up to? The shop's closed, I see.'

'Yesterday.' She grimaced. 'I handed over the keys to the Wilsons — Mrs Wilson grabbed them off me, I should say. She couldn't wait to get me out of the door. Now I'm unemployed, and looking for work.'

'You'll soon find something, Anna.'

'That's what everyone says. I'm not so sure, though.'

'You will.'

He stared at her a moment longer and then started back up the ladder.

'Bye, Matthew!'

'See you!' he called back over his shoulder.

She continued on her way, slightly disappointed he hadn't wanted to continue the conversation. She had always had a laugh with Matthew. Not today, though. He was busy.

She would have to get used to that, she thought wearily. Everyone was busy. She was the only one now with time for idle chit-chat.

She did wonder if anything was wrong with Matthew, in particular, though. He just hadn't seemed as cheerful as usual. In fact, he hadn't had much to say to her at all lately.

She wondered what she had done or said wrong that day he had taken her to Longwitton. There must have been something. She couldn't understand it. Such a lovely day they had spent together, too. But since then, he'd scarcely had a word to say to her.

She sighed. He was just busy, probably. Intent on his work. So he should be. He worked so hard. And now he was working on that old ruin of a house as well. Whoever had bought it was going to need an awful lot of money and patience to sort it out. It was bad enough on the outside. Goodness knew what the inside was like.

She spun round, hearing the clatter of hooves behind her.

'Carol!' she cried with delight, seeing her friend.

'Good morning, Anna. Just taking the beasts for a ride. There's a spare one for you, if you fancy it?'

Anna laughed and shook her head. 'No, thank you! You look far too high up there.'

She admired the three horses Carol had with her, the one she was riding and the two she was leading.

'That's a pity. Going far?'

'Just up to Dawson's Wood, and then along by the river.'

'Have fun!' Carol rolled her eyes and added, 'More fun than poor Matthew, anyway. Did you see what he's doing, back there?'

'I did. He wasn't in a very chatty mood, though. So I didn't get much out of him. Who's he working for, I wonder? Who's bought that old place?'

'No idea.' Carol shrugged and turned to check the horses she was leading. 'I must get on. They're becoming impatient with me. See you later!'

Anna waved her off. For a moment she quite envied Carol. At least, Carol still knew what she was doing each day.

Then she wondered if Carol could be why she had seen and heard so little of Matthew lately. She wondered if after the trip to Longwitton, Matthew had decided Carol was just right for him after all. Perhaps it was as simple as that?

⋆   ⋆   ⋆

'You would love it,' Don said to her one day when they were out for a walk.

'Would I? Would I really?' She smiled and said, 'Yes, I probably would.'

'So what do you say?'

'I'll think about it.'

They strolled on, crossing the dunes, heading for the beach. The evening was cold and clear. Cricket was being played, or practised, nearby but each man in the field looked like the famous advert for tyres, swaddled in multiple sweaters. It was an ambitious, optimistic harbinger of summer, even if the light nights were here again.

Don started off again. 'Come for a holiday. A couple of weeks, say. A month, even. See how you like it. We can take it from there.'

She had the time. The Wilsons had made sure of that. She even had the money to buy a ticket. That didn't worry her. But something else did. It was far too soon to be making any sort of commitment to Don.

'Where could I stay, if I did come?'

Don recognised her unspoken concern, and seemed easy about it. 'With my sister,' he said. 'She and her husband, Tom, have a lovely old home, with plenty of space. You've met Sally Anne. Tom's a nice guy, as well. They would be happy to have you.'

That seemed to answer her big question. She had met Sally Anne at the ceilidh, and once or twice since. She seemed very nice. Tom wasn't with her on this trip, but Anna was sure he would be nice, too.

'OK,' she said.

'OK?'

'I'd love to come for a holiday.'

He looked at her, laughed with delight and gave her a hug. 'I can guarantee you won't regret it. You'll have the holiday of a lifetime. And afterwards you won't be able to wait to get hold of that immigration application form!'

She laughed, too, but she wasn't altogether comfortable with Don's certainty. A holiday was one thing, but she wished he wouldn't go on so much about emigrating. She did like him, but he seemed to be expecting an awful lot of her.

If she did emigrate, she would be giving up so much. Everything, really. Everything she knew and was. And it wasn't as if they had known each other very long. Hardly any time at all, in fact.

Yet, and yet, was he really expecting, or asking, so much? What, exactly, would she be giving up here? No job, and not much prospect of one in the immediate future. No place of her own to live. Not much world travelling either, she thought with a wry smile. And hardly any exotic holidays at all!

Besides, Don was suggesting an initial visit only, a holiday. That was all. What was wrong with that? She could go and see if she liked it. She would also be staying with his sister, so there would at least be some kind of breathing space from each other.

But was he the one?

Perhaps. She was being cautious, but she did like him. A lot. Already she knew that. And the prospect of being with him for a couple of weeks, a month even, was thrilling to contemplate.

'Will I really like Calgary?' she asked shyly, knowing even before he answered what he was going to say.

The Adventure of a Lifetime

The journey and the flight, was just a blur. Yet exciting, too. Anna had never experienced such a long flight before, but it passed remarkably quickly. Most of the nine hours was spent flying over Canada, she was astonished to find.

The Atlantic turned out to be nothing like the gulf she had always thought existed between the two continents. What was it they used to call it in old wartime films? *The Pond*? She could understand why now.

Don and his sister, Sally Anne, met her at the airport. It took an age to get through security and customs, and everything else, but eventually she could see Don's smiling face on the far side of the barrier. Sally Anne was waving frantically. Anna blew them a kiss and waved back, and began to relax. She had made it. She was in the right place.

'Welcome to Calgary!' Don proclaimed, wrapping his arms around her and giving her a hug and a kiss.

She kissed him back and broke away, laughing. 'I can't believe I'm here! Hello, Sally Anne,' she cried, accepting another hug. 'Gosh! I'm really here, aren't I?'

'You're really here,' Sally Anne agreed, kissing her cheek.

'How was the flight?' Don asked.

'Wonderful. I really enjoyed it.'

'Even the food?' Sally Anne queried.

'Even the food!' Anna laughed again. 'The poor airlines. They get such criticism over their meals, but I think they do really well. The meals were lovely.'

'Better than they used to be, anyway,' Sally Anne conceded.

'What have you got in this thing?' Don asked, complaining about her suitcase. He had lifted it from the trolley, and promptly dropped it again.

'Hardly anything,' Anna assured him.

'It's nearly empty.'

'Empty, huh?'

'Come along, Donald!' his sister urged. 'Don't be such a wimp. Show her how strong a Canadian boy can be.'

Don grinned and took Anna's hand with his own free hand. They set off, Anna listening to the non-stop commentary on just about everything from Sally Anne, with occasional contributions from Don.

Within a few minutes they were loaded into Don's car and headed into the city. It wasn't far. The airport was on Calgary's northern edge.

'So that's it,' Anna said, when she saw the collection of high-rise towers ahead. 'Wow!'

'That's it,' Don agreed. 'Downtown.' He threw her a quick smile. 'Like it?'

'It's wonderful.' She shook her head and marvelled. 'It's just like all those pictures you see of American cities.'

'Except this one is Canadian,' Sally Anne said from the back seat. 'So it's better.'

'Yes, of course. I'm sure it is.'

'Just so you know,' Don said with a wink.

'We're hardly provincial at all here,' Sally Anne added.

'You two!' Anna said, laughing.

Twenty minutes later they were in the middle of it, the cluster of towers, and they were busily threading their way through the downtown. Don said they could have avoided the centre by keeping to the freeways but he wanted her to see it close up. Anna nodded.

She was tired, but she watched and observed with fascination. Everything was so different. The cars, the buildings, even the people at the bus queues and standing on street corners. She felt like pinching herself.

★ ★ ★

Sally Anne's home was in Bonavista, a 1960s suburb of big houses and bungalows set well back from wide roads, with manicured lawns and with water sprinklers going everywhere.

Sally Anne's was a two-storey house, white with black timbers creating a fake Tudor effect — except for the roof, which had purple tiles. A couple of giant blue spruces shielded the front of the house and a line of white birches edged the driveway alongside an immaculate lawn. The garage itself would have made a decent-sized house.

'Home!' Sally Anne announced.

'What a beautiful house,' Anna said, impressed already.

'It was,' Don said grimly. 'But just wait and see what the kids have done to it.'

'Your nephews and niece,' Sally Anne reminded him, opening her door. 'Our little angels.'

Don winked at Anna. 'Little monsters!' he growled.

They were anything but that, Anna soon discovered. They were two cheerful small boys, Jack and Lee, aged six and eight, plus Katy, a delightful ten-year old. Together with their father,

Tom, they were eager to greet their visitor from overseas. Even the obviously very popular Uncle Don had to take a back seat.

'Have you met the Queen?' Katy wanted to know.

'Not yet,' Anna had to admit.

Katy swallowed her disappointment bravely and announced that she had made jelly for supper.

The boys wanted Anna to come into the garden and play ball with them.

'Later,' their mother said firmly. 'Better yet — tomorrow. Or the day after,' she added in an aside for Anna's benefit.

Anna laughed as the children were shooed out of the kitchen. 'You're so lucky, Sally Anne!'

'What? Having these guys to chase around after all day?' The scowl turned to a grin. 'Yes, I am,' she conceded, ruffling Jack's hair.

Tom was a quiet, serious seeming man, some years older than Sally Anne. Anna put him in his early forties, and his wife perhaps ten years younger.

Like Don, Tom was a lawyer. And so was Sally Anne, Anna was surprised to learn. A qualified but non-practising lawyer.

'I gave it up when these guys came along,' Sally Anne explained. 'Maybe I'll go back to it when they're a little older. Maybe.'

'You'd better,' Tom said with a chuckle. 'By then, we'll need the money. We'll have some big school bills to pay.'

'Alternatively,' Sally Anne said, 'I could change my mind and stay home. Tom could just work harder.' Sally Anne winked.

'See how it is?' Tom said ruefully to Don. 'These women? They rule the roost.'

Don shook his head. 'How ever did you let things get this bad, Tom?'

'Get out of here!' Sally Anne laughed. 'Come on, Anna. Let me show you to your room.'

'I've taken your suitcase up, Anna,'

Tom called as the two of them set off.

Anna thanked him with a smile. Then she turned to follow Sally Anne. Already she felt she was going to enjoy her stay with these people.

After supper she began to feel the day catching up with her. The journey had taken a lot out of her, and it was, she knew, way past her normal bedtime even though it was still early here. Fortunately, her hosts were alert to the signs and understood the situation. They called an end to the evening and told her she needed to get her head down.

In a delightful bedroom with the scent of cedarwood all around her, she did just that. For a few minutes she tried to re-live the day. Then she gave in happily and embraced sleep.

Anna Meets Don's Friends

The next morning Don collected her after breakfast and they took off on a whirlwind tour of the city. Anna soon lost track of where they were, as they sped along freeways and parkways, and past commercial strips and shopping malls. She was overwhelmed. She didn't know where to look next.

Over coffee in a small cafe downtown, Don could see her confusion and he took pity on her. 'We'll slow down,' he said. 'We don't have to see everything at once.'

'No, no! It's wonderful.'

He smiled and placed his hand on hers. 'I can't tell you how great it is to have you here.'

She smiled back. 'And I can't tell you how good it is to see you again, Don. And all this!' she added with a flutter of her hand that took in all of Calgary. 'I can hardly believe it.'

'Oh, you ain't seen nothing yet!'

She grinned. 'Where next?'

'How about we drop by my place? Let you see where I live?'

* * *

Where Don lived was high up in a downtown apartment block. It wasn't a massive apartment. Just a big living room to go with a tiny kitchen, a bathroom and a couple of small bedrooms. Not a lot in it either. But pleasantly, easily done. Pale-coloured furniture, Scandinavian style. A few wall hangings. And a view — such a view!

Anna stood at the window, gazing down at the toy cars and buses edging along the streets, and the insect-like people crawling across the sidewalks and standing waiting patiently for transport. It was like gazing down into a beautifully constructed doll's house.

'I could do this all day!' she called

over her shoulder.

Don joined her. 'I never really notice any more. In fact, I don't spend a lot of time here, to be honest.'

'Just somewhere to hang your hat?'

'That's it.' He nodded. 'And somewhere to get my head down every night for a few hours. It's convenient.'

And that was how it seemed. Convenient. Minimalist living. Free of complications. Free of commitments. Leaving plenty of time to work, and to do the things that really mattered to him. Not a home at all, she thought. Don could collect his stuff and be out of here in twenty minutes, if he wanted. Matthew's old flat back in Callerton was more of a home.

'Do you maintain it yourself?' she asked.

'Maintain it?' Don chuckled. 'If anything goes wrong here, I move house immediately!'

'What about cleaning, laundry and so on?'

'I pay a service charge for stuff like

that. I don't have time for it.'

'I bet there are days when Sally Anne would like an arrangement like that.'

'I just bet there are.' He shook his head. 'That's what you get with kids, though — lots of work!'

She laughed. 'Other things, as well.'

'Oh, yeah? Worry, expense, trouble? It's better being an uncle than a dad, I reckon.'

'Said with feeling!'

He laughed. 'I'm sure Tom would agree with me.'

'I'm sure he wouldn't.'

'No, perhaps not. Ready for lunch?'

She glanced at her watch, surprised. It wasn't much after eleven.

'We lunch early in Calgary,' he explained.

'Why not?' she said. 'Where shall we go?'

'I thought we'd eat in.'

'Oh? You're a cook, too, like Tom?'

'No way! Come on.'

Eating in, she discovered, was done at the restaurant at the top of the tower.

'I don't do food,' Don explained. 'Just coffee. Otherwise, this little cafe here satisfies me.'

It was different, Anna thought, amused. Very different.

Matthew at least opened tins.

★　★　★

Afterwards they went to see Fort Calgary, where the city had begun life in 1875. That was a surprise. Anna was amazed by how young this huge city was.

'All this,' she marvelled, 'in not much more than a hundred years?'

'All of it,' Don assured her.

She did a mental calculation. 'My great-grandfather could have seen them lay the first brick,' she said.

'After he'd chased the buffalo and the indians out of the way. Sorry — First Nation, I should say, not indians.'

'Is that what they're called now?'

'Yep. We're very politically correct these days.'

She smiled. It was right, though, she thought. The settlers would have had to clear the land first. Buy the previous owners or occupiers out, or whatever they did in those days. Shoot them, probably.

'Didn't the Vikings have to do that in Northumberland?' Don asked, sensing where her thoughts were going. 'Cut off a few heads and ransack the place, before they could settle in?'

'I suppose they did,' she said with a smile. 'A long time ago. Otherwise we would all be Anglo-Saxons, or Celts even.'

'Can't stop progress,' Don said.

* * *

In the afternoon it was time to go to a barbecue some friends of Don's were holding, seemingly in Anna's honour.

'I'm not dressed for it,' she said uneasily, glancing down at her summer dress. 'Will I be all right?'

'You look just fine,' Don assured her,

taking her in his arms and kissing her.

'Really?' she said, smiling happily.

'Really! You look just perfect for a visitor from England. Nobody expects you to dress Western on your first day here.'

Visitor from England? Was that what she was? Yes, it seemed.

* * *

They were a good crowd at the barbecue. People in jeans, checked shirts and white stetsons. All ages. Huge quantities of meat smoked and sizzled on a big barbecue grid suspended over a charcoal drum. Crates of beer and soft drinks were piled high. Don steered her through the crowd, introducing her, letting people welcome her.

Anna soon stopped trying to remember names but she was overwhelmed by the open, friendly welcomes she received on all sides. Don smiled and encouraged her to relax and enjoy herself.

The hosts, Earl and Trudy, loaded

her with a plate of food and a large glass of something said to be 'tropical', juice, she thought. But there just might have been something with a bit of zip in it as well.

Then Trudy took her to one side to tell her where the facilities were, and how to reach them.

'Make yourself at home here,' she urged. 'We're very pleased you could make it. Besides,' she added, 'you're just what Don needs.'

Anna smiled uneasily. Was she? Was she really? And what, exactly, she wondered, was it that Don needed?

Earl took her over when Trudy was called away to some domestic emergency — a shortage of ice cubes, Anna gathered. Earl was a few years older than Don, and a true native Calgarian.

'One of the very few left,' he assured her. 'Most of these folks here today came ready-made from some place else.'

'Where?'

'You name it. Pretty much everywhere you ever heard of, and then some. Maybe not from your neck of the woods, though,' he added with a chuckle. 'Northumberland, England? I think you're a first.'

An Australian woman named Meredith told her it was great she could be here.

'Thank you,' Anna said politely. 'Have you been here long?'

'Five glorious years!' Meredith laughed and added, 'But I remember stepping off the plane, just like you, as if it was yesterday.'

A man from Ontario called Buck told her she had come to the right place. 'You'll love it here,' he said warmly. 'You'll soon adjust to the lifestyle.'

'I hope so,' she said, wondering if you really needed to do that for a holiday.

Earl and Trudy's house was a beautiful, old, two-storey timber building that Earl said his grandfather had built in the long-gone days before Calgary had become an oil centre. So the garden, and its many trees, had had time to grow and mature into what seemed to Anna more like a botanic garden than one of the domestic variety.

'Before they found oil,' Earl said, 'this was cattle country. In many ways it is still. At least, we like to pretend it is. But most of us just dress Western, if I'm being honest. We don't live the life. But Grandfather was the real thing, a true cattleman. He built this house in the city after he had made his money through ranching.'

'He retired here?'

'Retired? No, he never did do that. Those old timers just never knew when to quit. But eventually Grandma Maisie had had enough. She said she wanted to see something of city life before she died, and she made the old fellow build this fine house here. I guess it became their winter quarters in their old age. Nowadays, farmers spend their winters in Hawaii or Florida. Back then, they stayed closer to home.'

Don came to move her on. Earl headed for the barbecue pit — to roast another steer, as he put it.

'Legends of the West?' Don asked her.

She grinned. 'Such an interesting story.'

'Yeah. Earl's a lot of fun. Happy?' he added, eyeing her shrewdly

'Oh, yes! Everyone's so friendly.'

'It's just the way we are,' Don said. 'I told you you'd love it here.'

'There's just one thing, Don. I have the impression people believe I've emigrated, not just come for a holiday.'

'Don't you worry about that. It will all get straightened out.'

Still, she did wonder what he had told them about her.

★　★　★

Sally Anne and Tom arrived later, having first taken their older boy to soccer practice.

'Soccer!' Anna said with a smile.

'You must know it,' Tom insisted. 'You guys invented the game.'

'Of course I know it. It's just that in England we never call it that. We call it football.'

'Oh, well. Trust you Brits to be different.'

'Tom!' Sally Anne protested. 'If they invented it, they can call it what they like.'

Anna laughed. 'I never watch football anyway.'

'Really?' Sally Anne looked almost shocked. 'But you do play?'

'Me? No, of course not.'

'I do,' Sally Anne said. 'I play every week, every Wednesday afternoon.'

It was Anna's turn to register surprise. Even more so when she heard that soccer was a popular female pursuit, rather than a minority male interest.

'Your introduction to culture shock,' Don murmured as they moved on.

* * *

In the days that followed, Anna was surprised by how easily she and Don resumed their relationship. She had thought it might be difficult in a different place, a different country, to pick up with him again, but not a bit of it. They might never have been apart.

'Do you remember that evening we walked on the beach at Alnmouth?' Don asked.

'And it was so cold?' He chuckled. 'It was, wasn't it?'

Memories! Already they had memories of their early times together. She snuggled against him and felt his arms encircle her. She breathed in the scent of him and held her breath. Don gently squeezed and hugged her.

'What about it?' she asked moments later.

'About what? Oh, nothing, really. I was just thinking here we are looking out over water again.'

Reluctantly, she raised her head and looked through the windscreen out over Glenmore Lake.

'It's different, though,' she said, gazing at the high-rise buildings in the background. They were not far from the city centre, even though the lake was so huge. 'It's warmer,' she added.

'Only because we're sitting in a car!' Don chuckled. 'Come on. Let's walk.'

It was different, she thought as they set off along the lake shore, different in so many ways, but they weren't. They were just the same. She shivered with pleasure.

'Cold?'

She shook her head and turned to him, burrowing her face into his chest. 'Just happy,' she said shyly.

They had paused to look out over the water, where gulls swooped and hovered for all the world as if they were out at sea. Don stroked her hair gently with his finger tips. She felt his lips brush the top of her head. She turned her face up to him and waited for his lips to touch hers.

Everything is still so perfect, she thought dreamily. And we have a whole month together to look forward to.

★　★　★

'So what have you guys been up to?' Sally Anne asked. 'Anything exciting?'

'We've had a lovely evening,' Anna assured her.

'Lucky you! Tom and I don't do exciting any more. By the time the kids are in bed we're usually dead beat. It's in the tin marked coffee!' she called to Don, who was hunting for tea bags.

'Of course!' Don said. 'Why didn't I think of that?'

'So where did you go?' Tom asked in a quiet aside.

'The big lake,' Anna told him.

'Ah! Glenmore. Like it?'

'It was lovely. Beautiful.'

Tom nodded. 'We like to skate there in winter. Then, any time about now, we like to get our sailboat out on the water.'

Anna settled back to enjoy the rest of the evening. She and Don had not done anything Sally Anne might have considered exciting, but their walk by the lake shore had been just right for them. And now so was this peaceful end to the day, in this beautiful home with such good people.

* * *

Later, she walked out with Don to his car. 'Thank you for a lovely evening, Don, a lovely day, in fact! Another one, I should say.'

He smoothed her face with the tips of his fingers and gazed into her eyes. She smiled happily as she reached to kiss him.

'You OK here, with Sally Anne and Tom?'

'Oh, yes. They're very kind, both of them. And the children are such fun. I love it here. I love this house, too,' she added with a glance over her shoulder.

'It's all right, I guess.'

'All right! No, it's a lot better than that.'

'You'd like to live some place like this?'

'I would. I can't think of anything nicer.'

'Well,' Don said. 'One day we might.'

She smiled and let him go. She gave one last wave as his car turned the corner and he flashed his lights for her benefit.

Then she turned to go back inside. Somewhere like this, she thought with a wry smile. Was that really possible?

A Secret From Don's Past

'I do like your apartment,' Anna confided. 'I can't get over this view you have.'

Don joined her at the window.

'Look!' she said, pointing. 'Canoes on the river.'

'Kyaks.'

'There's a difference?'

'There sure is. I'll take you out on the river one day, and show you.'

'I'd like that.' She let him fold his arms around her, and pressed herself back against him. 'So much to see and do,' she whispered. 'A month may not be enough.'

'Stay longer. Stay forever.'

'With you?'

'With me.'

She chuckled and turned her head. Don wasn't laughing, not even smiling.

'Oh, you'd soon get tired of me,' she said.

'Never.'

'I'd be in your hair.'

'No, you wouldn't.'

'You'd have to cut down on your nights out with the boys — drinking beer, playing pool, or whatever it is you all do.'

'I'd find that easy.'

'Would you?' she asked, straining to see his face.

'Think of the money I'd save.'

'Oh, you!' She gave him a playful push and laughed at his rueful expression. 'Besides,' she added, 'I would want children, and that really would cramp your style.'

'Ah! That's a good point. I don't want to end up like poor old Tom.'

She laughed again and broke free. 'I knew you didn't mean it,' she said. 'You're just a typical male. Selfish and no sense of responsibility.'

'You know me so well.'

But she didn't think she did.

And she knew Don wasn't really like that. He was a wonderful man. She couldn't bear to think of the coming time when the holiday would be over, and they would no longer be together every single day.

'Shall I make some coffee?' she asked.

They were to spend time with some more of Don's friends that evening.

'Coffee would be good. You know where it is, don't you?'

'Of course.'

She knew this apartment so well by now, and if she didn't know absolutely everything about it she certainly knew where the coffee was kept

'The mountains look good tonight,' Don said. He was still standing at the window when she returned with two steaming mugs.

She peered into the far distance, and could just see them. Little bumps on the skyline, some sixty miles away. Perhaps eighty, Don said. Mostly you knew what they were because of the dark clouds gathered over them.

'Is it raining?' she asked.

He nodded. 'Or snowing, perhaps. We'll have to go out there. Let you see them.'

'That would be nice.'

Almost automatically, she had moved back close to him. Now he reached for her and she welcomed his arms encircling her. She hugged him back.

They kissed, and she no longer felt in foreign territory. They were back somewhere they had both come to know so well.

'I meant it, you know,' Don said, easing away.

'Meant what?'

'I wouldn't ever tire of you. You mustn't think that.'

She hugged him harder and closed her eyes. 'I don't really think that,' she admitted. 'Not at all.'

And it was true. She knew it was true, and she knew she felt the same way about him as he did about her. Perhaps they could start thinking of a future together? Why not? They were so good together.

'And I would never tire of you,' she whispered with a shiver, knowing she spoke too softly for him to hear, but knowing he would understand anyway.

'The coffee!' she said, breaking away with a smile. 'You shouldn't distract me.'

'You're easily distracted,' Don said with a chuckle. 'It's easily done.'

And she knew that was true, too, at least where he was concerned.

★ ★ ★

There was always something new to do, it seemed. Places to see. People to visit. Sunshine and blue skies to experience. Restaurants to try. Don took time off from work to make sure she saw, well, everything, really.

'How are they managing without you?' Anna asked. 'All this time away from work just to show me around.'

'Anna, you're the most important thing around here. While you're here, nothing else counts.'

'Oh, I bet you say that to all the girls!'

He shook his head and looked very serious. 'No, never. I'm not a party animal.'

She smiled and touched his hand lightly with her fingers. Then she turned and concentrated on the road ahead. And what a road it was. They were driving out to Banff, in the Rockies. Already the mountains were pressing in on them.

'Another half-hour,' Don said. 'Will you be ready for lunch by then?'

'I could be.' She glanced at him and laughed. 'So much eating and drinking! I'll have to avoid the bathroom scales when I get home.'

He shook his head and smiled. 'Not you,' he said.

★ ★ ★

It was lovely. Everything. Yet Anna wasn't entirely happy. No, she thought, that was wrong. She was happy. Very happy. Into the last week of her month's holiday now, and she had never had such a good time. Don was wonderful, and still they were so good together.

She was happy, she repeated to herself. Very happy. It was just . . . What? Well — oh, she didn't know!

It was all going so fast, too fast. And not only her time here. She had come for a holiday, and it was a brilliant holiday. But it was also something else, and she wasn't always quite sure about that. There were some big decisions to take.

Don seemed to assume her mind was made up now about emigrating, and perhaps about something else too. He hadn't actually asked her to marry him, but the question was there unspoken all the time.

And there was an assumption, an assumption that she would say yes when he did get round to asking her. She wasn't sure she was ready for that, not when she had her thinking cap on.

There was such a lot to consider. You had to think about it carefully.

Unless she was imagining it all, what Don felt? But she didn't think she was. It was the way he kept on talking, imagining, their future together. She felt sometimes as if she scarcely had any say in the matter.

So? What was wrong with that? She was very fond of him. Perhaps she loved him even. She wasn't entirely sure about that. But then, she chided herself, how could you be sure? How could anyone? Love, real love, surely had to grow on you, not arrive suddenly, unexpectedly in a blaze of fireworks from somewhere over the horizon.

But perhaps that was wrong, too? Perhaps love did just happen, with delicious surprise, when you first laid eyes on the special person with whom you wanted to share the rest of your life.

Or maybe it all depended on what sort of person you were?

So all she really knew, she decided, was that it was too soon for her to be certain, about anything.

But there was something else she knew — life with Don, life here, would probably be wonderful. It was just a little too soon, a little too early, to be taking such big decisions. He wasn't giving her time to think.

Still, he hadn't actually asked her yet, had he? She smiled. Perhaps she was going too fast, too. Perhaps she was reading too much into things. This was a different country, after all. They would do things differently here.

★ ★ ★

Banff took her mind off these questions that were looming ever larger in her mind. It was a pretty little town in the National Park, the main visitor centre for people from Calgary, as well as a global tourist centre. The mountains came up close, with their snow caps and their bare, white rock, and the dark forest on their lower slopes.

'Oh! It's so beautiful here,' she breathed.

Don smiled and said nothing, content with her reaction.

They wandered the streets for a little while, enjoying the air and the sunshine, poking into the craft shops and galleries.

Anna bought more postcards, these to keep rather than send. It was almost too late to be sending postcards home now. Then it was time for lunch.

'This little restaurant is my favourite,' Don told her, as he steered her through the doorway of a log cabin. 'For special occasions I always come here.'

Was this such a special occasion, she wondered.

They sat in comfortable wooden chairs with floral seat pads, elbows resting on an elbow-worn pine table. Anna gazed out into a street of timber buildings, many with verandahs and hanging baskets of petunias in full bloom.

'I feel as if we could have been doing this any time in the past hundred years,' Anna said whimsically. She smoothed the surface of the table with the palm of her hand. 'And how many people have done this, I wonder?'

'It's like a heritage centre, isn't it?' Don laughed. 'Probably you could have been doing this a hundred years ago — if it had existed then!'

'Oh, no! Don't tell me it's modern?'

'I think it is. Does that spoil it for you?'

She shook her head. 'It just makes it feel like we're on a film set. But it's still wonderful to be here,' she added, smiling.

And so it was. Such happy days they were spending together.

'It's been wonderful having you here, Anna,' Don said. He gazed at her and smiled. 'I can't wait for you to come back, for good.'

There it was again, the expectation, the assumption, that went further than she wanted at present. She tried to dismiss her concern.

'Oh, Don! It's been lovely for me, too. A perfect holiday.'

They got on so well together. He was a lovely man, and a wonderful companion. She did like him so much. But coming back, for good?

There was so much to consider. Too much at the moment. Why couldn't they take it a little easier, and reach that point at a pace that suited them both?

Don seemed to sense her difficulty. She hadn't said quite what he wanted to hear. But he just smiled and ordered coffee.

'Give me time, Don,' she said placing her fingers on his hand.

'Of course.'

'A holiday, however wonderful, isn't the right time to be taking such big decisions. We have to be sensible. One step at a time?'

He nodded.

There, they left it.

★   ★   ★

But Sally Anne didn't have any reservations or inhibitions about saying what was on her mind. That evening she sat with Anna after Don had dropped her off. Just the two of them.

The children were in bed. Tom was out late, playing pool with friends. Anna was happily tired and ready for bed, but she felt a need to talk to her host.

In truth, she hadn't seen a lot of Sally Anne. So she felt an obligation. Besides, she liked her. She had been so wonderfully kind and hospitable, as well as understanding.

'So have you guys got it all worked out?' Sally Anne asked over mugs of coffee. 'Dates, and everything? When it's to be — and where?'

'Whatever do you mean, Sally Anne?'

'The wedding, of course!'

Anna smiled, uncertain for the moment how to respond.

'You know,' Sally Anne added, 'you don't have to wait for the formal immigration procedures. Once you're married, you can just come and be here anyway.'

'I'm not sure we've thought that far ahead,' Anna said uneasily.

'Oh, you might not have, but Don has!' Sally Anne laughed. 'He's got it all worked out. He never stops telling me.'

So there it was, out in the open. She had begun to worry something like that was the case. 'There's a lot to think about,' she said carefully.

'And he's done it — believe me!' Sally Anne laughed. 'My little brother was always way ahead of the field. And let me tell you how happy Tom and I are about it. We're looking forward so much to having you as our sister-in-law. We didn't like the last one very much at all, but you're perfect!'

★   ★   ★

It was a long time before Anna found sleep that night. There was such a lot to think about. Too much, really. Don, marriage, emigrating. And now there was something new to add to the mix: Don had been married before, and had not told her.

Sally Anne had not said much about her brother's previous marriage, but enough to suggest that it had been a hasty, ill-conceived union that had never been made to last. Las Vegas had come into it, Anna gathered, both at the beginning and at the end. Don liked to play the wheels and the dice and the cards, and sometimes it worked for him. Other times, Sally Anne admitted with a sigh, well . . . The least said, the better.

But with Anna it would be different, Sally Anne added. She knew her brother, and she could read the signs. She knew this time it would be different, and so much better. One failed marriage didn't stop a person having a happy life subsequently. Didn't make him, or her, a bad person, did it?

Well, what was wrong with that, Anna thought afterwards, any of it? She liked Don so much. Perhaps even loved him.

And what a life he was offering! This was a wonderful city in a wonderful country. She had a lot to be grateful for. It was just — well, just such a breakneck pace he was setting. But she could get used to that, she thought with a wry smile.

Why not? Everyone else that had come here had.

So she would go home and sort things out, as she had said she would. Think about what she really wanted, and what would be best. She would be sensible, not carried away in the heat of the moment. Then she would give Don her answer.

Almost certainly she would tell him *yes*. And then they would go from there. Make the arrangements. Tick the boxes. Prepare for a new life. And try to forget he hadn't told her about something so important as his previous marriage.

So, finally, she had a plan, and could go to sleep. But she didn't immediately. Not for a long time, in fact.

An Explanation From Don

On a day when Don had to be in the office, and Sally Anne and her family were all out, Anna decided to walk to the nearest shopping centre. She needed to buy one or two more gifts to take home. Even more than that, she needed to walk.

She was tired of going everywhere by car. She felt as if her legs were beginning to atrophy through disuse. At home she walked every day. Here, scarcely at all, unless she and Don drove somewhere first.

It was hot that day, far hotter than it would almost ever be at home. Dusty, as well. Dust lay across the pavement and the road, and swirls of it billowed into the air every time a vehicle passed. There was grit still from winter, and what she assumed was topsoil from the prairies beyond the city limits.

The air was also full of traffic fumes. Cars and buses swept past, leaving behind their acrid scent. Soon her eyes began to sting. Sweat ran down her neck and back.

One or two drivers hooted at her and shook their heads as they sped past. It was because she was walking, she realised. No-one else was walking.

It took her half-an-hour to reach the shopping centre. Long before then, she regretted her decision to walk. It wasn't a comfortable experience. Easy to see why no-one else was walking. Even the high school kids all seemed to have cars.

The mall was air conditioned, and blessedly cool. She entered its shaded interior with relief and sought out a coffee shop, where she ordered a glass of juice and a coffee. Both together. No expense spared, she thought wryly. I, too, could be a high roller.

Then she sat for a while and quietly watched people and thought about things.

For once, she didn't feel so good. Her head ached and she felt sweaty. The walk, she decided. It hadn't been good for her. She should have known better.

No! That was ridiculous. She had walked a lot all her life. What nonsense! It was just a hot day, and uncomfortable.

Yet that explanation didn't do it for her. She stirred her cappuccino moodily. The truth was she wasn't altogether happy now she was alone for a day. Without Don, or Sally Anne and her family, she had no shield to guard her in this strange land, and it was a strange land. On her own, she was exposed to just how strange it was. It wasn't only the heat either. Or the travelling everywhere by car. Not any of that. She wasn't really sure what it was, but it wasn't any one, single thing.

The size of the city was a factor. Because everyone lived in detached bungalows with big gardens, this city of over a million people stretched forever. Hundreds of square miles of it! So it was hard to get outside it unless you drove for hours. She wasn't used to that. She wasn't at all sure she liked it either.

Then there was the people. Oh, they were lovely! They couldn't possibly be more pleasant and friendly, or hospitable. They just couldn't. And they spoke English, of a kind. But the endless optimism was at times wearing.

Everything here was for the best, the biggest, the most beautiful, the most perfect. Everything. It didn't matter what the topic was — climate, holidays, houses, mountains, lifestyle — everything was just so perfect.

The way people spoke and thought was wearing her down. There were times when she longed to point out that there were things they didn't have here, or things that were not perfect. Like what? Well, she thought with a wry smile, they didn't have the sea, did they?

They were the best part of a thousand miles from the nearest ocean.

Also, speaking for herself, she wasn't at all sure she would like to spend half the year indoors because it was so cold outside either.

Well, she would just have to get used to it. And she would get used to it, she supposed. She would get used to it all. If — when — she married Don, she would become like everyone else. Endlessly cheerful and happy — and rich!

There was another thing, too. What would she do here? Herself, personally speaking.

Oh, she would live in a big house and learn to drive a big car, she supposed, and have lots of beautiful things around her. But all of them would be paid for by Don. What would she herself contribute? How would she spend her time? Cooking and cleaning the house wouldn't be enough for her. Nor would looking after Don.

Don said she would get a job easily enough, but what sort of job? She didn't have professional qualifications.

160

She wasn't a lawyer or a doctor, like so many of his friends and colleagues, and their wives. She could work in a shop, she supposed, but having seen these big shopping malls, she wasn't sure how much she would like that. One of hundreds, or thousands? Her days spent in artificial light? It was a world away from what she was used to.

She would adapt, she told herself firmly. She would manage, and be happy. She would. She swallowed her doubts along with the rest of her coffee, and got to her feet.

★   ★   ★

There was another hurdle to be faced. She dealt with it that evening over supper.

Don was in full flow about some legal dispute occupying him at work. He told the tale with gusto. He told it well, making her laugh.

'So,' he said eventually, 'what's on your mind? Something's eating you.'

'You can tell?'

'I can tell. I'm good at my job,' he added.

That made her smile, too. 'Perry Mason?'

'I could be, in another life. In this one, unfortunately, I don't get to deal with unsolved murders. It's all property disputes with people trying to become oil millionaires. Still, it pays the rent. You were saying?'

She took a sip of coffee and decided there was no better time than now to tell him what was on her mind.

'Why didn't you tell me you'd been married before, Don?'

His brow furrowed. He gazed at her with surprise. 'Boy, you sure know how to wrong-foot a guy,' he murmured.

'That's not what I'm trying to do, Don. I'm just puzzled.'

'Who told you? My sister?'

She nodded.

'Old big mouth, eh?'

'That's not fair. Don't you think I have a right to know?'

'There's a time and a place. It's not her business.'

A chill swept through her. 'Sally Anne can't have known you hadn't told me, Don. Don't go blaming her for anything. She and Tom have been very kind to me this past month.'

'Of course they have. That's what families are for, isn't it?'

They seemed to be getting nowhere fast. It was like wading through treacle. 'You still haven't answered my question, Don.'

He shrugged and opened his arms with a gesture of surrender. 'What can I say? It just didn't seem important or urgent enough. Obviously I would have told you eventually.'

'Eventually?'

'Sure. When it needed mentioning. Come on! Your second last evening here. Let's enjoy ourselves.'

Anna wasn't quite ready to drop the subject. 'Tell me about her. Who was she? What went wrong?'

He sighed. 'She was from Toronto.

We met in Vegas, both of us on vacation there. We had a good time. So we tied the knot.'

Anna was stunned. 'So fast?'

Don shrugged again. 'It seemed right at the time.'

'But it wasn't?'

'Not really, not as it turned out. I guess we just wanted different things in life. End of story.'

It wasn't, of course. Not for Anna.

They went dancing soon afterwards. Some salsa club Don knew. Great atmosphere. Good music. Some fine dancers. People Don knew. Anna liked to dance, too, and did her best to enjoy herself. But a cloud had edged across the sun. She knew now there was even more to consider than she had thought. Maybe this, too, was just a holiday romance. How could you tell?

'She Thinks You'll be Emigrating'

Dad met her at the airport. 'You shouldn't have bothered,' she protested happily. 'I could have got a taxi.'

'A taxi, to where we live? It would be cheaper to buy your own car! How are you, anyway?' He examined her with a critical eye. 'You look well,' he concluded with a big smile, giving her a hug and a kiss.

'I am well! I've had a wonderful holiday.'

'That's good. Come on, then. Let's get out of here.'

He grabbed her case and led the way through the noisy, busy throng. She wondered where all these people were going. The airport seemed bigger and more crowded than ever.

'How's Mum?' she asked when they were outside, threading their way through the crowd waiting for taxis, buses and pick-ups.

'She's fine. Looking forward to you being back. She would have come with me, but there were things she had to see to. People!' He shrugged melodramatically. 'You know what they're like. Worse than cattle and sheep.'

Anna laughed. 'She's being busy, is she?'

'As usual. Visiting the sick and the lonely, the boring and the infuriating.'

'What would they all do without her?'

'What, indeed.'

The air was different, she realised as soon as they were outside. Not at all the same as in Alberta. It was incredibly moist, for one thing. You could feel the water in it. Cooler, as well.

In Calgary it had been sharply cold in the mornings until the sun got to work. Then it had soon become hot. Here it was chilly and damp. She could feel it on her face. It wasn't an unwelcome feeling. It was, well, familiar. She was home.

'Are you cold?' Dad asked, noticing her give a little shiver.

'A little,' she admitted. 'It's just the contrast. The plane was so warm. What's the weather been like here?'

'Normal,' he said, giving her a strange look. 'Cold and wet. It is June, remember?'

'Summertime.'

'You've been away too long.' He chuckled and added, 'Summer is that two warm days we sometimes get in July, in a good year. Remember?'

She laughed. Dad! Nobody had spoken like that in Calgary. There, nobody ever said anything derogatory about the weather, or anything else. Everything there was, well, perfect. Which it was, really, she supposed. At least in some ways.

They reached the car, which Dad had left in the short-stay car park for convenience.

'Expensive here?' Anna suggested raising her eyebrows.

'You know me. Last of the big-time spenders.'

She chuckled at the very idea. Home,

she thought happily, as he let her into the car and went to store her case in the boot.

Dad smiled at her when he got in behind the wheel. 'You seem to have been away a long time, love. We've really missed you.'

'I feel I've been away a long time,' she admitted. 'And I've missed you, too.'

'Well, it's good to have you back again, even if only for a short time.'

A short time? She wondered about that as they manoeuvred out of the parking area and headed for the exit. What were they thinking?

It wasn't just the air. The colours were different, too. As they headed north, the landscape looked incredibly, brilliantly green. The grass and the trees, they just sprang out at you. Around Calgary, the land had mostly been dead and dried-out looking from the long, cold winter, only slowly coming back to life.

Here, the grass had never stopped growing, through a winter incomparably mild. To Anna's eye, the landscape was a pleasant surprise. She had, she realised, lost her bearings for a while.

'One thing I should tell you,' Dad said. 'Your mother's worried about your relationship with this fellow.'

'Don? Why on earth is she worried? He's a lovely man.'

'She thinks you'll be emigrating.'

He glanced at her.

'Oh, well.' She smiled and gave a little shrug. 'Mum worries about everything. She always did.'

'That's true.'

He left it there, and she was pleased he did. He had given her something else to ponder. If only she wasn't so tired, she thought, she would ponder it. As it was, she just wanted to get home, go to bed and get some sleep.

* * *

Mum gave no outward sign of worry. She just wrapped Anna in her arms and hugged her.

'You look tired, dear. So you must

have had a very good holiday,' she said, without much logic but with every ounce of motherly common sense.

'Oh, I am, and I have!' Anna laughed. 'It's lovely to see you, Mum.'

'You, too, dear. Are you hungry?'

'Hungry?' She shook her head. 'A cup of coffee would be nice, though. Then I must get some sleep. I'm desperate for it.'

In her own room, in her own bed, she relaxed and felt safe and well. And comfortable. All the questions, spoken and unspoken, could wait until tomorrow, or this afternoon!

As she drifted off, she felt very happy. She was so glad to be home.

★ ★ ★

It was the next day before Anna got up for good. Before that, she slept a lot of hours, woke for a time, even ate, but always she returned to bed.

The next morning her long sleep was finally over. She woke soon after seven, her old time, and after some stretching and turning got up. It was time to face the day, and to see how Callerton had fared in her long absence.

Disappointingly, she saw none of her friends when she ventured out onto the street. She wandered along towards her old shop out of sheer habit. It was still there, and still closed up. Whatever the Wilsons were planning, it hadn't happened yet.

One or two of her former customers, elderly women, were out and about, looking just as lost as she felt herself. She had a quick word with them, and was touched to hear them say how much they had missed her, and the shop.

On her way back along the street, she approached the old ruined house where she had seen Matthew working just before she went away. Disappointingly again, she could see no-one there, but someone had done a lot more work on it in her absence. A new roof had been installed, to go with the new windows.

Was it all down to Matthew?

Then she stopped and stared. She couldn't believe it. The ground floor now had what she could only think of as a shop window. It couldn't be anything else.

She was astonished. What on earth was that about? Someone thinking of opening a shop in Callerton? Who? And what kind of shop? She shook her head. It made no sense at all.

* * *

Later, she called at the stables where Carol worked.

'Anna! You're back.'

Anna grinned happily. 'I am, in person.'

Carol dropped everything, abandoned the horse she was brushing and rushed over to greet her.

'Oh! How are you? How was the holiday? How's Don? When?'

Anna laughed and waved her to a stop. 'Yesterday morning,' she said. 'But

I've been in bed asleep since I arrived. I was exhausted.'

'I bet! Oh, it's so good to see you. Come into the cafe. I'll make us a coffee.'

'The cafe?'

Carol waved airily at the timber cabin adjacent to the stables. 'My cafe. My home from home.'

'Oh, that cafe!' Anna said, laughing. 'I thought for a moment something must have happened or changed while I've been away.'

'In Callerton? No way!'

The cabin was a cosy little place. Especially so in winter, when the little wood-burning stove was usually on the go. Anna flopped on to one of the scruffy armchairs Carol had rescued from somewhere, a redundant old people's home, probably, and watched her friend make coffee.

'It's great to be back home.'

Carol brought two coffee mugs to the little table beside Anna. 'But you had a good holiday?'

'Oh, yes! I did. The holiday of a lifetime.'

'Lucky you.'

'But it's still good to be back.'

'Here?'

'Here.' Anna nodded and suddenly felt more certain of that than anything else in her life. 'This is home.'

'I suppose it is, but . . . Oh, Anna, tell me everything! What did you do?'

They talked for a good long while. Anna told her as much as she could before her voice gave out on her. She only wished she had photographs ready to show.

'What about Don?' Carol asked at last. 'How was it?'

'Fine. He was very nice, very kind. And his sister and her family were too. They all were.'

'So?'

Anna laughed. 'What do you mean, so?'

'You know! What's going to happen? Has he asked you to marry him?'

Anna nodded. 'More or less.'

Carol laughed. 'That doesn't sound very romantic.'

'Yes, then. OK? Yes, he has. Now we've got to sort out the practicalities.'

Carol got up to give her a hug. 'That's wonderful news. I'm so pleased for you.'

It was wonderful news, Anna thought. It really was. But the practicalities were something else. They were going to take some sorting.

'What's going on with that old house?' she asked. 'The one Matthew was working on when I went away. It looks as if someone has decided to open a shop.'

Carol shrugged. 'I don't know,' she said. 'I've not taken much notice. You'll have to ask Matthew.'

She looked round as if seeking a clock.

Busy, Anna thought. Of course she was. Carol had a job to do. Better let her get on with it. Time to go.

'See you tonight?' she asked. 'Would you like me to collect Peggy, and us all go into Alnwick together for a meal? To that Italian, perhaps?'

'Oh, yes!' Carol said, giving her a quick smile. 'Let's do that. Celebrate your news.'

Somehow that idea didn't cheer Anna up very much at all. She just wanted to get back to normal.

Upsetting News for Anna

Peggy, of course, already knew. 'Congratulations!' She cried as soon as Anna appeared. Anna laughed. 'How did — ?'

'Oh, the bush telegraph works pretty well these days. The internet helps as well, of course. So are we celebrating?'

'We are. Tonight. With Carol.'

'Great!'

* * *

Peggy was still in good form that evening. She never shut up all the way to Alnwick. Anna was glad Carol was driving. Somebody had to concentrate on the road.

'I'm so looking forward to visiting my cousin plus old friends all the way across the big, old Atlantic,' Peggy started.

Anna laughed. 'The Atlantic? It's not

that big. Do you know, on the way there you spend twice as much time, and twice as many miles, flying over Canada than you do across the Atlantic.'

'Really?' Peggy said.

'Really?' Carol said. 'That's interesting,' she added, looking as if it was exactly the opposite. 'Now tell us what the shopping's like.'

* * *

Romano's was, as Peggy put it, comfortably crowded. That meant pretty well full, but without people queuing for a table.

'Lucky we booked,' Carol said.

Anna nodded. 'It's my treat tonight,' she added. 'To celebrate.'

'But I'm driving!' Carol wailed. 'How can I celebrate?'

Peggy thought she had the answer. 'We'll get the manager, erm, what's his name?'

'Romano,' Anna said.

'Romano, then. We'll get him to put

any spare wine in a bottle for you to take home.'

'Along with any left-over spaghetti,' Anna suggested.

'Of course,' Peggy said.

'Nice,' Carol said, glowering fiercely.

★　★　★

'What's Sally Anne's house like?' Peggy asked a little later. 'Is it wonderful?'

'Yes,' Anna admitted. 'It really is a beautiful house. Lovely big rooms. Two storeys, but with a basement as well. And a verandah at the front.'

'I can picture it,' Carol said. 'A rocking chair on the porch.'

'And one of those big swings that take two people,' Peggy added.

Anna laughed. 'Not quite. But near enough. They do have chairs on the front porch. Then, at the back, there's a big deck overlooking the garden. There's a barbecue set-up on that. And it's in a lovely area. Nice and quiet, in the suburbs.'

'Quiet?' Peggy said, sounding disappointed. 'How far from the centre?'

'About fifteen miles.'

'Fifteen miles!'

Now Peggy was horrified. Anna laughed and began to explain how far people travelled and yet stayed within the city.

'Where will you live?' Carol asked. 'In the city centre or on the edge? In a village outside even?'

'I don't know,' Anna admitted. 'We haven't discussed it. Anyway, they don't have villages. From what I saw, you either live in the city or on a farm.

'Don has an apartment in the downtown area at the moment. I imagine we'll live there for a bit, until we get sorted out. But it would be nice to have a house like Sally Anne's, with a lovely big garden.'

'A lovely big garden means lots of work,' Peggy pointed out.

'Well, she'll have nothing else to do,' Carol pointed out. 'Will you?' she added.

Anna shook her head. 'No, not at first.'

That was still something she wasn't happy about. She would have to do something, even if Don couldn't see why.

'Until the little ones arrive,' Peggy said with a sly glance sideways.

'Oh, that won't be for a while!' Anna said hastily. 'At least, I hope I'll get settled over there first.'

That was enough of that, she thought ruefully. They were getting into territory she hadn't explored herself yet.

Carol sighed. 'So when are you going?'

Anna shrugged. 'I'm not sure. There's a lot to sort out. It will take time, I expect.'

'But soon?'

'I hope so.'

Soon? She hadn't got that far herself yet. Everything really was so complicated. Her hope was that if she could get the next few days out of the way, and sort her head out, the way ahead would be straightforward. She could hardly tell the girls that she still hadn't given Don a straight answer yet.

Thankfully, the conversation moved on. There were other things to discuss. They ordered their meals. They enjoyed themselves.

But Anna was still distracted. She wondered if the big change in her life really would come soon. Perhaps it would. But there was such a lot to sort out in a practical sense. She had no idea how long it would take to arrange immigration, for example.

There were other things to sort out, too. Her parents needed to be told about her plans, for a start. Especially Mum.

Not forgetting, of course, that she had to talk to Don first. She had told him that she needed to take such a big decision only when she was back home. She didn't want to be rushed into it when she was in the midst of a wonderful holiday, and risk getting it wrong.

He had said he understood, but she had known he was disappointed. So she owed it to him to make her mind up and tell him. Don needed to know where he stood, as much as she did.

Peggy waved a glass in front of her face. 'Anna?'

She looked up at Peggy, who was on her feet. 'What?'

Peggy raised her eyes to the ceiling and pouted theatrically. 'What's wrong with this girl?' she demanded.

'Love,' Carol said. 'She's in love.'

'Can't answer a simple question,' Peggy grumbled.

'What do you want, Peggy?' Anna demanded, laughing.

'Would you like another glass of wine?'

'Who's driving?'

'I am,' Carol said. 'It's my car, remember?'

'In that case . . . ' Anna said, turning back to Peggy. 'Yes, please!'

'At last!' Peggy said.

'Has anybody seen Matthew lately?' Anna asked.

'Carol has,' Peggy volunteered.

'Oh?'

'Not since Sunday,' Carol said with a grin. 'Not for two whole days.'

It took a moment but then Anna caught the drift. 'You haven't . . . ?' she began.

'Oh, yes she has!' Peggy said.

Anna raised a quizzical eyebrow.

Carol laughed. 'I've been going out with Matthew, yes. Just this past few weeks.'

'Oh? I am pleased for you,' Anna said. 'I'm pleased for you both. How is he?'

'He's fine. Matthew is fine.'

But Anna wasn't sure she was. She felt as if someone had hit her very hard in the solar plexus. She scarcely had air to breathe, let alone speak.

'Has Don Asked You To Marry Him?'

Mum, of course, was anxious to hear what she planned to do. 'Have a rest, Mum. Catch up on some sleep, get used to me being back here.' She shrugged. 'See people.'

'That's not what I mean, Anna.'

They were sat at the kitchen table. Sunlight streamed through the window. Anna stared down the long garden at the back of the house. It looked beautiful. It always did at this time of year. There was so much colour in the borders. Perhaps later she would get out to do some weeding. There was always plenty to do.

She knew perfectly well what Mum meant. Of course she did. She just wasn't sure what to say to her.

'Has Don asked you to marry him?'

There it was, out in the open. She could evade the big question no longer.

'Yes,' she said, turning to her mother with a smile. 'Yes, he has.'

'I knew it!'

'Of course you did. I wasn't going to go all that way, for all that time, if it wasn't serious, was I?'

Mum looked so happy that Anna couldn't help laughing.

'That's wonderful news, dear! When is it to be?'

'When is what to be?'

'The wedding! Don't you play games with me, my girl.'

'I don't know yet. We haven't decided.'

'You don't know!'

'Well, there's a lot to consider. You know. It takes so much planning.'

'Of course I know! All the same. Where will it be? Here? Will we have to travel to Canada, because that would be wonderful too. How exciting!'

'Mum, can we just leave it for now? You're asking me questions I can't

186

begin to answer.'

Anna watched as her mum got up and moved across to the sink. She began washing up.

'Sorry, Mum!' Anna got up and moved behind her. She put her arms around her and hugged. 'I didn't mean to snap.'

'That's all right.' She glanced over her shoulder and smiled as she continued working. 'You're just back. You must be exhausted. And here I am asking you all these questions.'

Anna held on to her a moment longer. Then she squeezed. 'There's a lot to sort out,' she repeated.

'Of course there is, dear.'

Anna let go and returned to her chair.

'Where does Don stay exactly?'

'In the centre of the city. He has an apartment in a high-rise building. Wonderful views. But it's just for convenience. He says we would get a house somewhere. Like his sister's, probably. She has a lovely place in the suburbs.'

'I can't imagine living in the centre of a big city,' her mum said. She sounded almost wistful. 'It must be very exciting.'

Anna smiled. Exciting? Yes, you could say that, she supposed. People, traffic, shops, and so on. Very different to Callerton, anyway.

★   ★   ★

'What will you do yourself?' her dad wanted to know, when they were talking later.

'I'm not sure at this stage, Dad. I'll find a job doing something, I suppose.'

'She'll be busy building their home,' Mum intervened. 'Don't talk daft, what will she do!'

Dad looked dubious.

'And having a family,' Mum added, being very coy. 'Later on, I mean. You'll want that, won't you, dear? When you get settled.'

Anna gave her a wan smile that could have signified anything. What would she do? She had no idea. And the idea of having a family was far too distant a prospect to contemplate.

She shouldn't feel this hesitant about such an important part of her future, but somehow she just couldn't picture domestic bliss at the minute. What was wrong with her?

Her mother had simply asked a straightforward question, so why did she feel uneasy? Just nerves. It had to be.

Oh, I don't know, she thought wearily. I don't know what to do.

'Anyway,' Mum added, 'Anna won't need to work. Don seems to have a fine career.'

That was true, Anna thought. He did. And so did all his friends. Fine careers, every one of them. Their wives and partners did, too. That was a thought that didn't make her feel any better.

'And besides, you'll be busy enough clearing snow,' Dad said, giving her a wink. 'From what I understand, there probably won't be a lot of time for anything else in the winter out there. It can be pretty harsh.'

Anna smiled reluctantly, not hugely amused but relieved to have the conversation diverted.

* * *

One thing she particularly enjoyed about being back home was that she could walk. She walked everywhere. She walked and walked. The lanes around Callerton were wonderful, especially at this time of year. There was hardly any traffic, and the verges were like wild-flower gardens.

It was good to see the river again, too. The water level was high. Not in flood. Just high, the muddy, peaty water lazily drifting and swirling its way to the sea. She sat on the bank and watched the pattern of ripples and whorls on the surface.

Here and there she saw bubbles as fish came to the surface, looking for unwary insects. Two swans arrived, landing in mid-stream with a commotion that sent sheets of spray flying. Then they sailed gently away downstream together, as if on a summer excursion, not a care in the world.

Reluctantly, she re-focussed. She would give it another couple of days. Let things settle down. Then she would start making enquiries and doing the things she would have to do. She really ought to get on with it.

Moving to a big city would be a challenge. So would life with Don. But she was looking forward to it. Really she was. It was just that she needed a bit more time to get her head round it all. That was to be expected, wasn't it?

She would miss everyone here, though. She really would. Carol and Peggy, and everyone else. Mum and Dad, of course. And Matthew. People she had known all her life.

She thought about Matthew and Carol. How wonderful, she thought, now she had come to terms with the news. It was so good for both of them. What a happy life they would have together, if they stayed together.

She hoped they did, she decided firmly. Really she did. Matthew was wonderful. He always had been. Even at first school, when they were little, he had been so kind and cheerful. Always. Carol was very lucky.

Well, so was she herself lucky. Don was a lovely man, too. He led a very different sort of life to her, of course, but joining him and taking part in that life was an exciting prospect. She was going to do that, she told herself firmly. She couldn't wait.

She stood up and dusted the back of her jeans with one hand. Just as soon as she could, she would begin enquiries and start making arrangements. Her new life beckoned.

★ ★ ★

A few days after her return, Anna saw Matthew working on the old house

192

again. She went to see him.

'Hello, Matthew.' He turned towards her and nearly fell off the ladder. 'Careful!' she warned.

He slid down to the ground and straightened up. 'Hi, Anna. I heard you were back. Good holiday?'

'Yes, thanks. But it's good to be home. How are you, Matthew?'

'Oh, I'm all right. There's never much wrong with me.'

He grinned, but it wasn't the old Matthew, the one she knew so well. This one seemed oddly diffident, unsure of himself, unsure what to say to her. What was the matter?

Oh, rubbish! She had just been away too long. A lot could change in a month. A lot had changed, she thought, remembering what Peggy and Carol had said.

'So who's taken over this old ruin, Matthew? Who are you doing all this work for?'

'It's not much,' he said, again diffidently. 'Just the roof and the windows. A bit of pointing on the walls.'

'And a shop window, Matthew. Come on! I'm very curious. Who's taken it on?'

'Me,' he said after a long hesitation. 'I bought it.'

She thought she had misheard, and waited. He said nothing more.

'You, Matthew? Did I hear you right?'

He nodded and gave her a sheepish grin.

'Matthew Greig! What a bold step. What are you planning to do with it?'

He scratched his arm distractedly. 'I don't know,' he admitted. 'It just seemed a good idea at the time. The village needs a shop, doesn't it?'

He grinned again and started back up the ladder. 'I'd better get on,' he said. 'I have to be up at Kidlandlee by two o'clock. Some folks there want a fence to keep the wild goats out. That's going to be a challenge.'

'Good luck with it, Matthew!' she

called, as he reached the gutter and began working at a bracket holding it in place. He waved a hand in acknowledgement.

★ ★ ★

Afterwards she felt out of sorts. She had been about to tell Matthew how pleased she was for him and Carol, but somehow the opportunity had not arisen.

Matthew had not seemed ready to talk at any length with her. He had been busy, of course. You couldn't expect him to drop what he was doing just because she had returned from holiday. He had work he was doing, and another job to go to afterwards. He was a busy man. Always had been.

And now he seemed to be embarking on a new enterprise. Understandably, he had not wanted to say much about it. He would want to make sure everything was in place before he started broadcasting his plans from the rooftops.

That was part of the trouble, she thought moodily. Matthew had plans. Carol had plans. She was sure Peggy had, too. Plans and jobs. Everybody did.

And herself? Well, if not plans, exactly, she thought firmly, she certainly had things to do. She had a new life to prepare for. First, though, she ought to tell Don her answer. Nothing else could go ahead until she did that. She would phone him. Tonight. And tell him. Then make a start.

By then, she was along by the river again. She looked up. She stood and gazed around. How peaceful and beautiful it was here, she thought, seeing it as if for the first time.

The two swans were back, she noted, as they would be. After all, they were partners for life, which was exactly how it should be. This time they were foraging in the reeds not far from where she stood. They took absolutely no notice of her. It was their world, they implied. She was welcome to enter it but on no account must she even think of interfering or disturbing it.

Smiling, she stood still and watched. They were so busy. They became even busier when two grey signets appeared and demanded to know what was going on.

Their parents showed them, with patience and care. And with love, she realised. They, too, had their place in this little world where permanence and continuity underlay everything else. It was her world, too, when you thought about it, Anna thought. It was where she belonged.

Eventually she turned away. Still smiling, she set off for home, ready for lunch, and knowing now exactly what she wanted to do. It was easy, after all, once you knew what was right for you.

She would phone Don this evening, she reaffirmed, her mind finally and absolutely made up.

★ ★ ★

Don was slow to respond. She waited patiently. 'You're sure?' he asked.

'I'm sure.'

'There's no way I can change your mind?'

'None at all. I'm sorry, Don. But I know now it wouldn't be right for either of us.'

They spoke some more, awkwardly, hesitantly. She apologised again. Don was very well-mannered about it all, disappointed but polite.

There were no ugly reproaches. Nothing like that. Anna was relieved. She hoped he would come to see she was right.

'I guessed,' he said finally. 'I realised I should have known better when you didn't grab my hand off.'

She chuckled. 'Oh, Don! We had a lovely time together. Thank you so much for that, and for being so understanding now.'

'Just one thing. Was there anything in particular that led you to your decision?'

'No, nothing like that.'

There was, of course. It was the

swans. When, and if, she married, she wanted to do it for the right reasons, and she wanted it to be for good, in the place she considered home. Perhaps it wasn't a very modern thing to think, but she knew it was what would be right for her.

Not that she could tell Don any of that. He had his own way to find in life, and it wouldn't be the same as hers.

'Take care, Anna!'

Afterwards she felt free as the proverbial bird. She went out and almost skipped down the street. It was done. Decision taken. She had her life back.

* * *

Peggy was disappointed, predictably. Carol just seemed stunned.

'I'm so sorry,' Peggy said immediately. 'How awful. How sad!'

'No, it's not. I'm more relieved than anything else.'

'Are you? Really?'

Anna nodded.

'There go my holiday plans,' Peggy said with a theatrical sigh. She looked round Romano's, where they were once again, ostentatiously searching for a new holiday plan. 'Are you sure?' she added, turning hopefully back to Anna.

'I'm sure.' Anna gave a little shrug. 'I don't want to live in Canada. I'm happy here. Besides . . . '

'Besides what?'

Anna hesitated. She wanted to express herself precisely, and not risk being misunderstood. 'Don is a lovely person. So kind and pleasant, and thoughtful. Such good fun, too.'

'Is that a big *but* I hear?'

Anna smiled and nodded. 'I think you know when someone is not right for you. At least, I do.'

'But you could live in such a lovely house!' Peggy said. 'Drive a great, big car. Wonderful holidays. No money worries at all!'

Anna laughed. 'The cars are not so big these days. Relatively speaking, of course.'

'Still ... Oh, you're so hard to please! If anybody like that asked me, well. I would be on the first plane to Canada.'

'Oh, shut up, Peggy! You know you don't mean it.'

Peggy pouted and then grinned.

Carol had been quiet so far. Now she said, 'Well, I'm glad you weren't swept off your feet entirely, Anna. I should have known, I suppose. You're far too sensible for that. You always were. Not like me.'

'My great failing,' Anna conceded ruefully.

She almost meant it. Peggy was right. What a lifestyle she could have had, if only she had chosen it and swallowed her doubts about Don.

On the other hand ... It couldn't possibly have lasted. Perhaps Don didn't know that, but she did. Perhaps Sally Anne did, too. It had been a holiday romance. No more, no less. Now she wanted to tuck it away in a little box and get on with her real life.

'What will you do now?' Peggy asked.

'Look for a job. Think about finding somewhere to live on my own. Mum and Dad will be thinking they're never going to get rid of me.'

'Maybe we could look for somewhere together?'

'Maybe we could. Yes. That would be nice.'

She turned to Carol, who was strangely quiet. 'I've been meaning to ask you, Carol, what is Matthew intending to do with a shop?'

'No idea.' Carol shrugged and added, 'Ask him.'

It seemed an odd thing to say. Ask Matthew? Her? It was hard to believe Carol hadn't done that herself.

'I will, if I see him. I just thought . . . '

She stopped as Carol got up and walked off, presumably to the Ladies. She glanced at Peggy, who shrugged.

'What?' Anna said. 'What did I say?'

'Oh, it's not you,' Peggy said wearily. 'She's out of sorts, depressed.'

'Why?'

'Because of Matthew.'

'What's he got to do with it?'

'Between you and me, I think he's dumped her.'

'Oh, dear!' Anna was stunned. 'Poor Carol. I didn't know.'

'She'll get over it.' Peggy shrugged again, and added, 'Fortunes of war, I guess. Something like that anyway.'

'You've Ruined My Life!'

Anna saw nothing more of her friends for a few days. Peggy worked in town. So not seeing her was no surprise. But Carol was around. She had to be, because of the horses. Occasionally Anna saw her in the distance, riding or leading her charges, but she always disappeared before she could talk to her. And the once or twice she went round to the stables, Carol wasn't there. Busy, she supposed. Like everyone else.

Now, though, Anna could give some serious thought to her own situation. She, too, wanted to be busy, and there was no reason to delay job hunting any longer. The sooner she got started, the better.

The job centre in Alnwick didn't have much to offer, and what vacancies they did have on their books were not very enticing. Anna didn't really feel she wanted to be a temporary clerical assistant at a sausage factory, still less a mechanic. As for being a part-time fryer at a local chip shop, well, no, thank you.

'I would rather be a brain surgeon,' she told the woman behind the counter. 'Or a footballer. They earn heaps of money. Haven't you got any vacancies?'

The woman shook her head. 'Sadly,' she said, 'we don't have much of anything at the moment. Not that we ever do,' she added. 'That's how I ended up in here myself.'

'Oh? They took you on?'

'Temporarily. Frankly, I can't wait to retire or be made redundant.'

'Good luck,' Anna said, chuckling.

★　★　★

What she would really like to do, she thought over a coffee in a local cafe, was what she used to do. She had spent years running a village shop all on her own. She would like something like that again. But where would she find it?

She hung around Alnwick until it was time for Dad to pick her up on his way home from work.

'Any luck?' he asked.

She shook her head. 'No, not a thing.'

'You'll find something.' He glanced sideways at her as they drove up the long hill leading out of town. 'Early days yet.'

'Yes,' she said. 'I know.'

She knew, but it didn't stop her feeling dispirited.

'I assume you've quite made up your mind about the other business — emigrating, and getting married, and so on?'

'Oh, yes.' She smiled at the way he had put it, as if it was all on a par with a visit to the dentist's. 'I don't want to do any of that. I'm happy here, or I was, and I will be again once I find a job.'

'Of course you will.'

They drove on. Dad started whistling. That got on her nerves.

'Dad! You don't have to do that.'

'Do what?'

'Whistle to keep up my spirits. You don't have to do it. I'm all right.'

'Of course you are.' He grinned. 'Tell you what. I'll get you a puppy. How would that be?'

'Dad! Stop it. Stop it now. I'm really not depressed. I just need to get sorted out.'

He relented. 'All right,' he said with a smile. 'So what would you like to do?'

She sighed. 'What I would like to do is what I used to do before the Wilsons pulled the plug, but that's not going to happen, is it?'

Dad was quiet for a couple of minutes. Then he said, 'Why don't you have a word with Matthew Greig? See what he's going to do with the old Robson place. I see he's put a shop window in.'

She was stunned. Somehow, in all the upheavals, she hadn't thought of that. Matthew! Yes, what a good idea.

★ ★ ★

'How are you, Carol?' Anna asked her friend. Things were incredibly strained it seemed.

'All right. You?'

Anna chuckled. 'Getting a bit fed up of job hunting, but OK otherwise.'

They had met outside the Co-Op in Alnwick. Anna was glad to have met someone she knew. 'Fancy a coffee?' she asked.

'No thanks. I've got things to do.'

Carol looked thoroughly miserable. Anna felt sorry for her. 'Are you sure you're all right? You don't seem very happy.'

'Happy!' Carol looked to be about to say something else, and then changed her mind.

'What is it? Is there anything I can do?'

'Go back to Canada! Have you thought of doing that? You've ruined my life.'

Anna was stunned. Carol looked angry for a moment. Then her expression became sullen again.

'Carol! Whatever's wrong? What have I done? I can't believe you just said that.'

'You mean you don't know?' Carol said, glaring at her.

Anna shook her head, bewildered and fearful. 'What is it? What's wrong?'

'Matthew.'

'Matthew? What do you mean?'

Suddenly Carol was in tears. Instinctively, Anna put her arms round her, hugged her and drew her aside. 'Carol,' she murmured. 'Come on. What is it, hinny?'

Carol sobbed for a moment or two. Then it stopped and she straightened up. 'Sorry,' she murmured. 'I'm so sorry.'

'It's all right. Come on. Let's go somewhere and sit down.'

They found a quiet little cafe, and a quiet corner within it. Anna bought a couple of cappuccinos.

'I usually have latte,' Carol said, staring at the glass mug with the swirl of cream. 'Skinny latte.'

'Something else I've got wrong, then,' Anna said with an anxious smile.

Carol shrugged. 'Sorry. I wasn't thinking. It's not really your fault anyway.'

'What's wrong with you and Matthew?'

'Nothing.'

'You can't just say that. What is it?'

Carol sighed and moodily stirred her coffee.

'You have to tell me. What have I done?'

'You? You came back.' Carol forced a grim smile. 'You decided not to emigrate, not to marry Don. I don't know! Since you came back, I haven't seen Matthew.'

'What's that got to do with me?'

Carol gave a bitter little laugh. 'You mean you don't know?'

Anna shook her head.

'You really don't know?'

'Of course I don't. I've scarcely seen either of you.'

Carol muttered something and took a sip of her coffee. A smear of cream appeared round her mouth.

'What did you say?' Anna queried, passing her friend a tissue.

'It's you he's interested in, Anna, not me. It always was.'

Anna stared at her a moment. Then she smiled awkwardly. 'Don't be silly! He's never even looked at me. We've known each other since we were children.'

'I'm not being silly. I mean it. It was all right when you were going away, marrying someone else. Now you're not doing that, and it's not OK.'

Abruptly, Carol stood up and headed for the ladies. Anna watched her go.

She was dazed, and trying desperately hard to understand what Carol had just said.

It made no sense. Matthew interested in her? He never had been. All the times she had seen him, and talked to him, all the time she had known him. He'd never once given any indication whatsoever that he was romantically interested in her.

No, that was wrong. He had taken her to Longwitton that day. And then he'd dropped her. That had been it. One day of his company. That was all.

'You're wrong,' she said when Carol returned.

'I'm not, you know.' Carol made an attempt at a brave smile. 'Come on! I've got the boss's Land Rover. I'll give you a lift home.'

'Are you sure?'

'Of course I am.'

Anna got to her feet.

'Cheer up,' Carol said. 'I'm all right now. And you're not really to blame.'

'She Doesn't Really Blame You'

Carol, in just a few words, had given Anna such a lot to ponder. Part of her was sorry for her friend's troubled mood. Part of her didn't believe what she had heard. Yet another part of her wanted it to be true, even though she knew it couldn't be. What to think? What to do about Matthew?

As she walked back along the street to Physic House she was startled by the screech and squeal of a vehicle pulling up alongside her. She spun round to see Matthew's old pickup, with its piles of fence posts and rolls of barbed wire in the back.

Matthew leapt from the cab, called a greeting and immediately dropped to the ground and disappeared beneath the truck. She could see his boots sticking out as he began to hammer away at something. She waited.

'What was that all about?' she asked when he emerged.

He grinned. 'You wouldn't believe it, would you?'

'What?'

'This old truck has been all over the hills today, and it waits till it's travelling slowly along a flat, tarmac road to break a spring — badly, as well.'

She shook her head and smiled. 'No, I would never believe that, Matthew. Not in a million years. It must be fate.'

'There you are, then. Fate.'

He pulled off his raggedy jacket and tossed it into the cab.

'You should look after your clothes better,' she said. 'It'll get all creased, treating it like that.'

'So if I folded it carefully and laid it down gently, the holes and the oil stains would disappear, would they?'

'Possibly.'

'Yeah. Possibly. That's what I think, as well.' He laughed and shook his head. 'When do you go back to Canada?'

'I'm not.'

'Not what, not going?'

She shook her head.

'What about that bloke, Peggy's cousin? I thought you were getting married?'

'What about him? And what about Carol?'

'Seriously?'

She nodded. 'Seriously.'

The grin left his face. He weighed something up and then said, 'There's a few of us going over to Longwitton tomorrow night. It's my Uncle Dick's Coming-Home Party. Do you want to come?'

'It's his what?'

'He's coming home from hospital. We thought we'd throw a little get-together for him.'

'A coming-home-from-hospital party? That sounds fun.'

'Yeah.' The grin was back. 'Doesn't it? Better than a staying-in-hospital party anyway. But it will be all right. It's in Gordon's shop,' he added, as if that clinched it.

'Oh? The Village Shop, eh? That's different.'

'So?'

'Thank you, Matthew.' She smiled, and tried hard not let anything else show. 'I'd love to come.'

'Pick you up at six. Not in this, though.'

'That's a pity.'

Matthew grinned. 'We've got a mini-bus.'

'I can't wait.'

Still smiling, she watched as he roared away in his lopsided truck, which was now down in one corner because of the broken spring. Like old times, she thought happily. The same old Matthew. She gave a little shiver.

★ ★ ★

'I'm sorry about you and Don,' Mum said, 'but I have to say I'm glad you've changed your mind about emigrating.'

Anna smiled. 'So am I. It wasn't right for me. None of it.'

'If that was what you really did want, I wouldn't have stood in your way or tried to make you change your mind.'

'I know you wouldn't.' Anna gave her a hug. 'But thank you, anyway.'

'I'm still glad you're not going, though.'

Anna laughed now. 'Drop it, Mum! It's over. Don't worry any more.'

'Oh, but I do. I can't help it. It's what mothers do. They worry all the time about their children. Anyway, where are you going tonight, if you don't mind me asking?'

'I don't mind at all. Don't be silly. A few of us are going over to Longwitton with Matthew Greig. It's a little party they've organised for his uncle. He's just come out of hospital.'

'Oh? Is that Dick Cummings?'

'Yes, I think so.'

'Nice man. Wish him well for me.'

'I will.' She considered for a moment. 'You all know each other, don't you? Matthew's Aunt Dorothy knew straight away who you and Dad were, as soon as

I said my name.'

'Dorothy Charlton, that will be. Before she was married, I mean. Yes, we all know each other. You're right. It's a small world, round here. We all went to school together.'

Anna thought about that as she got ready to go out. It was a small world. Mum was right. And that didn't make it a bad thing. Not at all. Quite the opposite, in fact, so far as she was concerned. She didn't want to live in a vast city, where everybody was from somewhere else.

This was exactly what she wanted, a small world where people knew and cared for each other. Just like this, in fact. It wouldn't suit people like Don, perhaps, but it suited her perfectly.

She dashed out when she heard the mini-bus arrive. Matthew was driving.

'Room for one more!' he called. 'Find a seat, if you can.'

She was surprised how many people were aboard. She knew them all, of course, and laughed and joked as

218

people greeted her.

'Take no notice of Matthew!' Peggy called. 'I've kept you a seat.'

Anna sat beside her and glanced around. 'No Carol?'

'Afraid not, no. She didn't want to come.'

Anna wasn't sure how she felt about that. It might have done Carol good. On the other hand, she was relieved. Besides, an out-of-sorts Carol wouldn't have helped cheer Uncle Dick up very much.

'She's all right,' Peggy said quietly. 'Don't worry about her. She doesn't really blame you. She'll come round.'

Anna nodded. 'I hope so,' she said.

★   ★   ★

The Village Shop in Longwitton was ablaze with lights and decorations. Even as she got out of the bus, Anna could see a throng of people through the glass door. Music hit her as she followed Matthew and Peggy inside.

Gordon met them. He was wearing what looked like a chef's hat and holding a glass of red wine. 'Welcome!' he called to all of them.

Anna grinned and said, 'Does the hat mean you're doing the cooking, Gordon?'

'Only some of it. Hello, Anna!'

She pressed on to be met by Kay. 'Nice to see you again, Anna. But didn't Matthew tell me you'd gone to Canada?'

'Only for a holiday. I'm back now.'

'Oh, that's good. He did miss you, you know.'

'Who did?'

'Matthew, of course. Who do you think? One of your other admirers?'

Anna laughed and allowed Kay to lead her away to meet Uncle Dick, who was a very large man with a very red face and a happy smile.

'I'm very pleased to meet you, pet,' he said, taking Anna's hand for a moment.

'I'm pleased to meet you, too. Last

time I was here everybody was worried about you. It's good to see you looking so well.'

'I'm as well as can be expected,' he said gravely. 'No better, no worse.'

'All things considered?'

'Exactly.' He winked and added, 'When you came last time, were they trying to work out where I kept my money?'

Anna giggled. She was saved from having to respond by the arrival of Matthew.

'We couldn't find it, Uncle Dick,' Matthew said. 'Not a penny.'

'And do you know why that is?'

'You haven't got any?'

'That's right, son. I've spent it all. Why not? They tell me you can't take it with you.'

Matthew looked glum for a moment. Then he said, 'How did the health MOT go? Are you good for another five hundred miles?'

Anna's surprised giggle soon became open laughter.

Uncle Dick said, 'It went well. They fixed my ticker, my knee and one or two other things, as well. They reckon I'm good for another ninety thousand miles now.

'Anyway, enough of this modern music,' he said, looking round. 'It's my party,' he added with a grin. 'They should be playing music I like.'

'Of course they should,' Anna agreed. 'What do you like?'

He didn't hear her. He had turned to follow Matthew.

Anna smiled at Peggy, who had appeared at her side. 'Help yourself to food, Anna. There's plenty on the table over there. Where are those two off to?'

'I'm not sure. But Uncle Dick wasn't happy with the music.'

Peggy pulled a face.

'So what does he like?'

'Elvis,' Peggy said with a smile. 'Come on!'

They made their way towards the food table as the music changed and Elvis Presley began complaining about somebody who was nothing but a hound dog.

* ⋆ ⋆

Later, Kay took Anna aside to tell her she was expecting a baby.

'Oh, how wonderful! Congratulations. So the party is for you and Gordon, as well as for Uncle Dick?'

'Not really. We didn't want to spoil his night, but — well, yes it is, in a way,' Kay admitted happily.

'I'm so pleased for you,' Anna told her.

Later still, she danced with Matthew. She was enjoying the evening so much, and even more so when the music slowed and he held her close.

'Matthew Greig!' she whispered dreamily. 'How did this happen?'

'So you're not emigrating?' he said in her ear.

'No.'

'You're not getting married either?'

She shook her head. 'Not as far as I know,' she said.

'Good.'

'Good?'

He smiled and let go of her as the music stopped.

Later still, dancing a waltz to another of Uncle Dick's favourites, Matthew sang along with the music, 'It was always you from the start.'

Anna smiled. 'Are you singing to me, Matthew Greig?' she whispered.

'I am,' he said. 'It was always you from the start.'

'Stop it!' she said, pushing him away playfully. 'You know you don't mean it.'

'Oh, but I do. Didn't you know?' he added, looking quite serious now. 'Marry me, Anna?'

'Yes,' she said without a moment's hesitation. 'Of course I will.'

Then he kissed her.

'I've Always Loved You, Anna'

The next morning Anna couldn't believe half of what had happened the night before. Had she imagined it? Some of it, at least? Probably. But she felt good about it, whatever had happened.

More than that. She wanted to see Matthew again, as soon as possible. She wanted to see him in the cold light of day. She needed to know if she had imagined it or if they really had said those things to each other last night.

He was waiting for her. When she left the house Matthew was there, sitting on the wall next to the gate, swinging his legs, whistling. Her heart fluttered.

'Have you got no work to go to, Matthew Greig?'

'None that can't wait,' he said.

He stood up, smiling, as she approached.

'Matthew Greig,' she said softly. 'What are you doing here?'

'I came to see you.'

'Oh?'

She smiled as he took her in his arms. She looked up to be kissed.

'I wanted to be sure,' he said afterwards. 'About what we said last night. I wanted to know if you'd changed your mind.'

'I'm sure,' she said, hugging him. 'I haven't told anyone yet, but I'm very sure. You?'

'I've always loved you, Anna. Always. *It was always you from the start*,' he crooned. 'But you never looked twice at me.'

'Oh, Matthew! That's not true.' She sighed. 'I'm shy. That's all. I never thought you were interested in me. I never thought you could be.'

He hugged her. 'Walk with me?' he suggested.

'Wait till I get my cardigan.'

She trotted down the path, opened the door and grabbed the cardigan she hadn't thought she would need.

Mum appeared in the kitchen doorway. 'Going out?'

'I am, yes. See you in a bit.'

'Is that Matthew Greig you were talking to?'

'No. It was the milkman.'

'The milkman? We don't have . . . '

'Bye, Mum!'

She slammed the door and sped up the path.

'What are you grinning at?' Matthew asked.

'Mum being nosey. Where are we going?'

Matthew said nothing. He took her hand and they set off.

'I wonder if Uncle Dick enjoyed his party last night as much as we did?' she said.

'Oh, he did. He was well away.'

'Quite a homecoming. Your auntie was enjoying herself, too.'

'She was. Gordon and Kay did well for them both.'

'They had something to celebrate,

too. Did they tell you?'

Matthew nodded and smiled. 'It was a happy night for us all.'

Anna smiled, too. She couldn't have agreed more.

They walked on until they reached the old building Matthew had been working on. They paused there for a moment and gazed at it.

'My goodness, Matthew! I wouldn't have believed how nice it could be again. You've put in an awful lot of work.'

'Aye.' Matthew nodded. 'Do you want to see inside?'

'You've been working on the inside, as well?'

'Just a bit. New floors and ceilings. Re-plastered the walls. New wiring. Kitchen. Bathroom.'

'Everything, really!'

'Just about,' he admitted.

She was impressed. 'There must be an awful lot of people waiting for their new fences, if you've been doing all this.'

Matthew laughed and led the way to the front door.

'I like this shop window, as well,' Anna said, pausing to study it. 'Is somebody interested in the shop?'

'They are, yes. I think I've found someone wanting to take it on.'

She felt a moment of disappointment. Oh, well. Served her right for not asking about it earlier.

She followed Matthew inside and began a tour of the interior of the building. There was nothing in it yet, but it was immaculate. Everything was new, just as Matthew had said. It smelled new, too. Walls and floors, and everything else. Three bedrooms and a couple of other rooms, all on the first floor.

'Downstairs is all for the shop,' Matthew said. 'Storage, space for the freezers, and so on. Up here is the living space.'

'It's lovely, Matthew.' She shivered. Then she turned, looked around and shook her head with awe. 'Wonderful.'

Matthew walked over to the window of the room they were in and gazed down the length of the unkempt garden. 'Plenty of work out there still,' he murmured.

'Whoever's taking the shop on is very lucky. Who is it, Matthew?' she asked.

He turned to her and smiled. 'You, I hope.'

'What?' She stared at him. 'Me, did you say?'

He nodded. 'I hope so.'

It took her a moment. 'Me?' she repeated.

'You,' he said. Then he sang the line from Elvis they had heard so much the previous night, and even once that morning already. 'It was always you from the start.'

She gave a little squeal and threw herself at him. Laughing, he held her tight.

'All this, Matthew,' Anna said dreamily. 'Why didn't you say anything?'

'I'm not really sure. At first I thought maybe you wouldn't be interested.

Then I just wanted to get it done before I showed you.'

'To surprise me?'

He nodded. 'That, and before I asked you.'

'Oh, Matthew!'

She buried her face in his chest. Then they began to dance. They moved slowly around the big empty room, their shadows dancing with them across the bare walls. They danced to the music in their heads, and with the love in their hearts.

★   ★   ★

The next month was busy. Anna and Matthew worked like proverbial Trojans, fitting out the shop and making all the other arrangements needed before the door could be opened to customers. There were suppliers to be contacted, credit lines arranged, samples to inspect, and visits to be made.

For Matthew, there were nails to be hammered, screws to be screwed, and fittings to be sought and bought. It was desperate, frantic work, but immensely exciting, too.

Anna felt as if she had been re-born. She had come alive. She poured all her energy, and all her knowledge and experience, into creating the business that was to serve everyone in Callerton, as well as themselves.

Somehow she and Matthew also found time for themselves, and their future together.

That evening at Uncle Dick's party had, it seemed, opened the floodgates. There was never any question now that their future was to be together.

'I'm so happy, Matthew,' Anna said one evening as they walked along by the river. 'I've never been happier, or more exhausted!'

Matthew laughed. 'Me, too,' he said. 'I tell you what, though. Shop work is killing me. I'll be glad to get back into the hills when you're up and running.'

That would be a while yet, she thought, but as soon as the shop fitting was done Matthew would be able to attend to his main business. He had plenty of fences to build, more than ever it seemed.

'What will we call the shop?' Matthew asked.

Anna had already thought that one through. '*Wooden Heart*,' she said without hesitation.

'You can't call it that!'

'We can call it what we like,' Anna said airily. 'And Gordon's already collared *Village Shop*. We need something different.'

'Yes, but people won't understand.'

'So they'll ask questions, Matthew, and they'll talk to each other. Good publicity, and it's free! Besides,' she added shyly, 'We will always know what it means, and where the name comes from. Perhaps your Uncle Dick will, too.'

Matthew looked puzzled for a moment. Then he got it and began to laugh. 'Why not!' he said.

She grasped his arm and pressed

her forehead hard into his shoulder. 'You're a good man, Matthew Greig,' she whispered softly.

He didn't hear her, but she knew he felt the same about her. They were lucky, both of them.

*　*　*

Mum said, 'I'm so glad you and Matthew have got together. I'm so very happy for you both. When are we going to start planning the wedding?'

Anna smiled. 'Soon,' she said. 'But first we've got to get the shop opened. We've got to start earning money instead of just spending it.'

'Quite right, too,' Dad said. 'Money doesn't grow on trees.'

Mum swotted him with a rolled newspaper. 'You old skinflint! It certainly doesn't grow on our trees. I've never seen any money since the day I married you.'

'Was that the worst day of your life, Mum?' Anna joked.

'Easily! By far.'

Dad pulled her to him and Anna beat a retreat, laughing. She hoped she and Matthew would be as good with each other.

A New Beginning

The day came. Anna proudly hung an OPEN sign on the shop door and stood back nervously. Would anyone come?

She needn't have worried. If the sign hadn't done the trick, the flyers she and Matthew had pushed through letter boxes might have done.

Or the announcement they had pinned on the village notice board. And if none of that had worked, one thing was sure, people would have known anyway. Word of mouth was still a viable technology in places like Callerton.

Even the Wilsons came to see what was happening. Anna was relaxed and offered them a cup of coffee. They both declined, Mr Wilson graciously.

'You've got it lovely, Anna,' he said. 'I hope you do well here. The village will have missed you since the old place closed.'

'Thank you.'

Mrs Wilson, not surprisingly, was pessimistic. 'It's hard to make a living with little shops these days,' she said with a sniff and a frown.

'We'll just have to work hard, Mrs Wilson,' Anna said with a smile. 'Matthew and I are both good at that. And how is retirement suiting you, can I ask?'

Mrs Wilson gave her an uncertain smile.

*　　*　　*

Later, much later, when opening day was over, they had another party, one to which only the two of them were invited.

'A perfect day,' Matthew said.

Anna nodded. 'Everything's perfect now,' she said softly.

Somewhere nearby music started up. 'I know this song,' Anna said, glancing at Matthew's little recorder.

They gazed at one another a moment, smiling happily, and then they both began to sing, 'It was always you from the start.'

THE END

We do hope that you have enjoyed reading this large print book.

Did you know that all of our titles are available for purchase?

We publish a wide range of high quality large print books including:
Romances, Mysteries, Classics
General Fiction
Non Fiction and Westerns

Special interest titles available in large print are:
The Little Oxford Dictionary
Music Book, Song Book
Hymn Book, Service Book

Also available from us courtesy of Oxford University Press:
Young Readers' Dictionary
(large print edition)
Young Readers' Thesaurus
(large print edition)

For further information or a free brochure, please contact us at:
Ulverscroft Large Print Books Ltd.,
The Green, Bradgate Road, Anstey,
Leicester, LE7 7FU, England.
Tel: (00 44) **0116 236 4325**
Fax: (00 44) **0116 234 0205**

ALL ABOUT ADAM

Moyra Tarling

Teacher Paris Ford hopes to improve the performances of Brockton College's basketball team. But going to the new athletic director for help, she's confronted by the startlingly handsome Adam Kincaid. Years ago, Paris secretly witnessed Adam's role in her family's scandal and she isn't about to forgive or forget. However, Adam's tender kisses melt her resolve to maintain a professional relationship. Now she must discover the truth about Adam's past and look toward a future . . . with the man she loved.

NASHVILLE CINDERELLA

Julia Douglas

In Nashville, thousands of talented people hope to make the big time . . . Starstruck Cindy Coin came from Alabama, but still works in Lulu's diner, alongside Tony — who's yet to make his mark. Hank Donno, looking every inch the successful manager, hopes to find his big star — then wide-eyed Katie arrives. And travelling on the Greyhound, Texan Jack just hopes that Nashville is ready for him. Can hopes and dreams be realised? And is romance in the air in Nashville?